Without warning, Kane's long fingers found her chin.

She glanced up but the shadows over his face didn't give her any clues to his thoughts. He simply covered her lips with his.

This simple touch sent her over the top.

He didn't grope or force his tongue into her mouth. No, Kane wasn't an overeager boy looking for an easy in. Instead, he rested against her mouth for a moment. Just long enough for her to anticipate the next move.

When it came, it left her gasping. He brushed his lips lightly across hers, back and forth until hers parted. Still he didn't force himself in. Instead he traced the outline of her lips with his tongue...and everything inside Presley tightened in response. One quick flick against her parted teeth, then he was gone.

Only then did Presley realize that her entire awareness had narrowed to the man touching her. The man she should have been scolding. But no—

She clutched the lapels of his suit jacket, wrinkling the fabric. She strained to draw air into her lungs like a horse bellowing after a race.

And the man before her stood with his hands loose at his side, appearing completely unmoved.

"See? Nothing to worry about."

Dear Reader,

Don't you just love when life doesn't go the way the characters anticipate? Let me share a secret with you. As an author, it can be a lot of fun! The hero in this book, Kane Harrington, has always directed his own life. I feel for him—I'm a control freak myself. Kane has learned that anything outside of his control will only bring pain and suffering. He's under the delusion that the heroine is under his complete control.

Too bad that love doesn't always play fair...

I love to hear from my readers! You can email me at readdaniwade@gmail.com or follow me on Facebook. As always, news about my releases is easiest to find through my author newsletter, which you can sign up for from my website at www.daniwade.com.

Enjoy!

Dani

DANI WADE

——

UNBRIDLED BILLIONAIRE

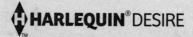

Recycling programs
for this product may
not exist in your area.

ISBN-13: 978-0-373-83853-0

Unbridled Billionaire

This edition published by arrangement with Harlequin Books S.A.

For questions and comments about the quality of this book, please contact us at CustomerService@Harlequin.com.

Printed in U.S.A.

www.Harlequin.com

Dani Wade astonished her local librarians as a teenager when she carried home ten books every week—and actually read them all. Now she writes her own characters, who clamor for attention in the midst of the chaos that is her life. Residing in the Southern United States with a husband, two kids, two dogs and one grumpy cat, she stays busy until she can closet herself away with her characters once more.

Books by Dani Wade

Harlequin Desire

His by Design
Reining in the Billionaire
Unbridled Billionaire

Milltown Millionaires

A Bride's Tangled Vows
The Blackstone Heir
The Renegade Returns
Expecting His Secret Heir

Visit her Author Profile page at Harlequin.com, or daniwade.com, for more titles.

To my beautiful baby sister ~ Following our dreams runs in the family...never give up on yours!

One

"You can take me on a stroll through the gardens..."

Kane Harrington glanced toward the large arched windows along the back hall of Harrington House, darkening from gray to black as the sun disappeared. "I don't think there's quite enough light for that."

The little imp—Joan was her name, if he remembered correctly—sidled a little closer. "I don't mind."

I do. And so did all the eligible women and their mothers who had hoped for a few minutes of his time. After all, he was the only Harrington man who was still single. That made him the center of attention at this open house for the new estate and stables he and his brother, Mason, were holding for prominent local families. Suddenly the four hours he'd already endured started to wear on Kane.

"I'm sorry, hon," he said, trying to infuse his normally stern expression with a sincere regret. "I just remembered I need to make a business call tonight. I'll be right back."

He quickly escaped down the hall to the large office they had marked off-limits during the earlier tours. Though Kane had his own desk and computer to work from in the office, he didn't live at the estate with Mason and his fiancée, EvaMarie.

Thankful for the heavily carved door that kept out unwanted visitors, he dropped into his desk chair with a squeak of leather and a sigh. His sudden exhaustion reminded him of why he had been avoiding social events over the last few years. To his eternal consternation, his dark, brooding looks seemed to attract the attention of more women than he wanted. And as soon as word spread that he and his brother had inherited enough money to be labeled billionaires, the number of potential wives chasing him had become obscene.

He'd agreed to take one for the team if his mixing and mingling got their newly established stables noticed by pretty girls and their families. Money wasn't the only thing they needed to keep building—although his father had ensured that they had plenty of that. No, they needed to build a reputation among the movers and shakers of racing society here in Kentucky bluegrass country. Kane would do whatever he had to in order to ensure their names were on every pair of lips at this year's biggest events surrounding the race to the Triple Crown.

After he'd had a few minutes to himself...

What surprised him was how utterly boring he found the women here today. The newly minted billionaire was looking for a bit of a challenge, a sassy remark or, hell, anything outside the cookie-cutter norm…but he hadn't found that yet.

And the fake helpless act…he shuddered. Kane had more protective instincts than most men, but he could see right through to the calculating performances that did nothing more than turn his stomach.

Idly, he clicked on his email icon and glanced over the notifications. The usual mix of ads, business replies and such filled the screen. Geesh—it didn't matter how often he checked his inbox; the thing just kept filling up.

Suddenly the name Vanessa Gentry caught his eye, and his world went still for long, long seconds.

He recognized it, of course, even after several years. *Kinda hard to forget the woman who would have been your mother-in-law.* Immediately his mind's eye filled with a picture of her with her daughter, both of them laughing, heads close together. They'd looked so much alike, only Vanessa's dark hair had gone silver gray at an early age. Her daughter Emily's had still been black as night. Just the thought saddened Kane.

Though he probably shouldn't, he clicked on the email and read it while a photo began downloading.

Kane, I know it is presumptuous of me to send this to you. But after the way things ended… Well, I just wanted you to know that all is well and that Emily has been able to move on.

Kane braced himself, straightening his spine against the back of the chair. Sure enough, as he glanced down at the picture that appeared, it was as though someone had landed a blow square in his solar plexus.

There she was, the beauty he'd thought to one day call his own. Odd—he'd thought he would never stop loving her then. Now love wasn't the emotion he felt. No, instead it was the familiar wave of weakness, the helplessness that had first plagued him during his mother's illness and death from cancer. Then Emily had had her accident, which sent all his fix-it instincts into overdrive. But she'd wanted none of his help. She'd interpreted it all as pity.

Beside her in the photo was an average-looking man, nondescript except for the tux and boutonniere. There was a happy glow in his eyes. Over Emily's shoulder Kane could see the handle of her wheelchair. So she was still at least partially paralyzed...

And a beautiful bride to someone who could apparently meet her needs better than Kane, no matter how hard he'd tried.

The anger hit quick and hard. Even though he didn't want to, Kane conceded that Emily had a right to move on. But Kane had a right to be left out of it, instead of being reminded of all the ways he hadn't measured up.

Surging to his feet, he ignored the slam of his chair against the wall behind him. Stalking across the expensive carpets without a thought, he continued out the door and down the hall without acknowledging the few guests he passed. He imagined his facial expression wasn't particularly welcoming at the moment.

The way people fell back as if he were the beast at the ball only confirmed his thoughts—and exacerbated his anger.

But his body knew what it needed. The peace and quiet he'd always found in the stables. The acceptance of the horses. The earthy smell that grounded him in the present. And today, the realization of the dream he hadn't been willing to give up—even after his ex-fiancée had fallen off her horse and been left paralyzed for life.

There was no one in the stables. They'd allowed tours earlier. After all, this would be the heart of their operations. Kane and Mason were rightfully proud of the building, the renovations they'd done here and the stock they'd started housing in the stalls. As soon as he entered, Kane's steps slowed, his breath evened out, his heart rate returned to normal.

He paused, savoring the quiet shuffle of horses' feet and their gentle calls to him as they sensed his presence. This time when he moved forward, his footfalls were almost silent. He was meditative as he strolled through the space. It was the realization of a dream he and his brother had for so long: premium-grade stables and the stock to one day race a championship horse.

He only wished his father had lived long enough to share it with them.

A sudden high-pitched squeak broke the silence. Then he heard a voice coming from the right-hand fork of the aisle. Kane wasn't as alone as he'd thought. Had a sneaky couple decided to play some games in the stables while the party was going on? Normally he would just ignore it, but that wing had been declared off-limits to visitors earlier in the day.

Because that's where their new breeding stud was being kept.

Sun was a very new addition, having only arrived yesterday, and Kane hadn't wanted him disturbed by a rush of onlookers. The horse needed time to get used to his new digs.

Picking up speed, Kane rounded the corner and made his way toward the noise. The closer he got, the more his calm melted away, because the voice seemed to be coming from the stud's stall. Singular and soft, it had to be a woman's. Either she was talking to the horse or some man was getting an earful of sexy whispers.

The stall was about halfway down the aisle, but as Kane approached, something farther down caught his attention. The back door to this wing sat ajar, giving him a glimpse of the black night…and the glint of the stable lights off metal. A truck? A trailer?

Was this woman stealing his horse?

His big body automatically adopted stealth mode, his feet almost silent on the hard-packed earthen floor. He gave the stall door a wide berth, coming around it in the shadows across the aisle so he could see without being seen. As he paused, a sudden awareness of the pumping of his heart and an intense curiosity flooded over him.

He wasn't bored now.

Over the half wall, Kane could see the massive stallion standing unusually still, almost as if mesmerized by the woman's voice. She spoke continuously as she worked—from what Kane could tell since she faced away from him, she was indeed readying Sun for transport. But the whole time she touched him, steadying him with a firm hand that bespoke familiarity and authority.

She wasn't dressed to steal a horse. Through the barely open door Kane caught a quick peek of the flat soles of the woman's sandals. The straps across her feet were bejeweled; he could see them peeking out through the straw. A loose sundress of nondescript gray-blue material skimmed her lightly muscled body instead of hugging her curves.

Her back was to him, but from what he could tell, she was pretty but not flashy. She certainly hadn't caught his attention earlier tonight. If she'd been present at the party—as the dress suggested—he couldn't remember her. And he had a feeling he would have remembered the wealth of caramel-colored hair pulled back into a thick ponytail. He wanted to see what her face looked like, but first, he needed to know what she was up to.

Many people didn't realize that behind his stoic exterior, Kane was an exceedingly patient man. He stood for a good ten minutes in silence, cataloging the woman's movements and actions, guessing at her intentions. She had an incredible talent for soothing the giant horse they'd nicknamed the Beast, but the breakaway-style halter, blanket and leg wraps on the animal left no doubt that she planned to leave here with his horse.

As if the truck and trailer didn't make that plain enough.

As she finished the last of her preparations, Kane decided it was time to make his move. Stepping out of the shadows, he moved to block the open stall door. The Beast caught sight of him first, lifting his head with a little jerk that conveyed his uneasiness at Kane's appearance.

The little thief didn't catch on as quickly. She placed her palm flat on the horse's neck and spoke to him in a low voice. He whinnied, seeming to nod, though Kane wasn't sure if it was in agreement or to warn her of his presence. Without a sound, Kane leaned against the door frame and let his sternest stable-manager voice boom out into the silence.

"What have we here?"

The voice jolted Presley's system. She'd been so caught up in Sun that she'd forgotten the threat posed by the Harringtons. One look over her shoulder told her she'd been caught by one of the actual brothers rather than a stable hand.

Remembering the papers in her pocket, she raised her chin and turned to face him fully. "I'm Presley Macarthur. And you are?"

She already knew. After all, Kane Harrington had made the social pages a few times already, though his brother, Mason, had appeared many more times…and would probably garner a precious full-page spread after today's announcement of his engagement to EvaMarie Hyatt.

She could recite the entire story of the stable hand brothers who had moved away from here after their jockey father had been blackballed, only to move back last year after inheriting a huge sum of money upon their father's death. They were set to make a big splash in the horse racing world.

The giant of a man loomed in the doorway, letting the silence stretch, but she refused to give in with a rambling explanation of what she was doing here. That would only make him think he had power—which he didn't in this situation.

Pushing away from the door frame, Kane stalked closer. "I would think, since you're in my barn, stealing my horse, that you would know who I am."

A sudden return of the heated anger and embarrassment Presley had felt when her stepmother had told her what she'd done with Sun had Presley's sight dimming momentarily. "Actually, I'm not stealing anything. I'm simply collecting what's rightfully mine."

"I don't think so, little girl," Kane said, his chuckle skating over her nerves in an unfamiliar way. There was an undercurrent signaling more to his attitude than mere disdain. A whole lot more she didn't want to acknowledge.

Kane went on, "You see, I have the paperwork that shows I bought this horse, fair and square."

Presley felt Sun shift his big body next to her, as if sensing the gist of the conversation. She rested her palm against his withers. "Fair? Are you sure about that?" she asked.

Kane's only response was to lift a darkly arched brow. Her stomach dropped, but she kept her expression as blank as possible. The intimidation she felt in the face of his stoic self-assurance was new to her. She'd been dealing with men—and their attitudes when they realized a woman was in charge—for many years now. Fear was foreign to her in a business setting. Yet this man evoked it with a simple look.

Not good.

She swallowed hard, but the fear got the better of her. "If those papers don't list the seller as Presley Macarthur, then I'm afraid you've bought this horse illegally."

Yikes. Presley immediately wished the words back. That wasn't the tack she'd meant to take. All the calm preparation she'd done before coming here was flying out the window. "What I mean is, there seems to have been a misunderstanding—"

"I'd say so. Because I bought this horse from the home farm run by the late Mr. Macarthur's widow, Marjorie."

While I was out of town on a consult...

"I'm sure you did, Mr. Harrington." Boy, that name was hard to force out from her constricted throat. "But it's a matter of public record that Sun is owned by me, Mr. Macarthur's only daughter. *Not* his widow." She smiled as sweetly as she could fake. "Though we do own the business jointly, so I can see where such a misunderstanding could occur."

The sudden brooding look he shot her made her want to stammer, but she fought for control. Reaching into the side pocket of her skirt, she pulled out a copy of her ownership papers. "If you need proof, I have it right here."

To her consternation, he stalked forward. Though she knew he was coming for the papers, her heart sped up and her palms grew damp. Once more she knew it

wasn't all from the stress of this situation. This felt…
personal. His long fingers brushed over hers as he took
the pages, and a hot flush spread like wildfire through
Presley's limbs.

What the heck was happening here?

Granted, Presley wasn't one to swoon. She was too
busy taking care of business. But she could honestly say
she'd never reacted to a man the way she had to Kane
Harrington. It felt as if a tornado had taken up residence
inside her body, swirling her emotions and reactions
into a maelstrom she couldn't control—or even make
sense of. As Kane read over the papers, she had a brief
reprieve to compose herself before he pinned her with
his gaze once more.

"Well, it seems we are at an impasse, Miss Macarthur."

"No." She drew the word out as if he were a child in
need of instruction. "This situation is very clear-cut.
I'll be taking Sun home, where he belongs."

"And the check I gave to Ms. Macarthur?"

Presley struggled not to wince. "I assure you, your
money will be returned to you in full." No matter how
much of a hit the business took because of it. Presley
had a sneaking suspicion her stepmother had spent as
much as possible before Presley could get wind of what
happened.

"And what about my reputation?"

She cocked her head to the side, tightening her hand
around Sun's lead rope. "Excuse me?"

Kane stepped closer, close enough to cast a shadow
over her. "I bought this particular horse for a reason,

Miss Macarthur. I'm sure you are fully aware of the jump start a stud of this caliber would give to our breeding program. That's not the kind of thing I can find just anywhere."

"I do understand, but don't really see where that is my problem."

But one look from Kane Harrington told her he was about to make it her problem. "I think the people around here would disagree with you."

"What do you mean?"

"We both know our businesses," he said with a smooth confidence. "We know they run on reputation almost as much as the performance of our horses."

Oh, Presley knew all about that, having experienced the struggle to keep her stepmother out of the business of running their stables since her father's death more than six months ago. Her stepmother didn't know the meaning of tact or, hell, even business. All she saw were dollar signs, and she wanted more and more—no matter what she hurt in the process.

They can scent a weak link better than a hound dog and will extort it worse than a lawyer. Never let them see weakness.

Her father had repeated those words to her again and again, so why had he decided that his daughter and his wife should *share* the business he had worked so hard to build since before Presley was born? Her stepmother was the weakest link of all—and Presley had a feeling Kane Harrington knew that all too well.

Wielding his power without noticeable effort, Kane moved closer, then had the gall to pace around her, making her temperature rise. The urge to move away became unbearable.

Just as Kane reached her back, she slipped beneath Sun's neck, putting the horse between them to avoid the unfamiliar arousal this man evoked deep inside. Yes, as much as she hated to give the feeling a name…

Kane's thick, dark eyebrows rose, but he didn't call her out on her cowardice. "The way I see it, your stepmother has done something illegal. And then there's the embarrassment of retracting the announcement that Sun would be joining the Harrington stables." He loomed over the horse's high back, pinning Presley with a steely-eyed glare that should have made her mad but instead sent intriguing shivers up and down her spine.

"If my reputation is gonna take a hit over this, so is yours," he assured her.

Anyone who thought the customer was always right had never been in just this situation with just this man. One look told Presley she was about to make many concessions—whether she wanted to or not.

Two

Kane could tell the moment Presley Macarthur realized he wasn't letting her off the hook without consequences. She was pretty good at hiding her expression—but her gorgeous, moss-green eyes gave her away.

They told him she was going to try to get out of this somehow.

"I'm really s-s-sorry about that—"

Kane shouldn't be happy about that stammer, shouldn't wish it was from more than just the pressure he was bringing to bear. It marked him as a bad person, surely. But it didn't stop the satisfaction from rushing in. The curiosity.

Whoa. This game is fun.

"So you're sorry your stepmother made a mistake. How do you plan to make it up to me?"

Only as her eyes widened did he realize how that might sound—and not just the words. An attraction, a need sparked by this woman had given his voice a husky quality. He hadn't had this type of reaction with a single debutante since he'd moved back to Kentucky.

Hell, years before that, even.

Why this particular woman? She wasn't flashy like the diamond-studded princesses in the main house. Her dress was pretty enough, made of a nice-quality material, but its loose style didn't reveal a single curve. Kane was intrigued by what might be waiting underneath for him to discover. And this close, he noticed another significant difference. Whereas every woman he'd met tonight wore makeup to a greater or lesser extent, Presley Macarthur's face was clean and clear, without so much as tinted lip gloss to highlight the sexy curves of her naked lips.

Suddenly her gaze narrowed, and she pulled herself a little taller. "What do you mean, exactly?"

The pushback intrigued him, too. The last thing he wanted was a weak woman, one who needed taking care of—that type was his kryptonite, as Emily had proven all too well. Before him was an attractive woman who obviously knew and ran her own business. If the gossip he'd heard was correct, Presley also did consulting on equine and stable management. So she was smart, not easily intimidated. Kane was going to have to get creative to recoup this loss.

He shook his head, ignoring her question while he worked out the puzzle in his head, well aware his silence would be intimidating in and of itself. What was happening to him? First his earlier anger. Now he was contemplating…what?

Blackmail?

Sure, that would get him a long way toward acting on this attraction, toward finding out what was beneath Presley's loose dress. *Not.* The sudden idea that popped full-blown into his head was very naughty. As if reading his thoughts, Presley leveled a suspicious gaze squarely in his direction. Kane relied on his instincts, but he wasn't usually quick to act. He thought things through, weighed the consequences, made plans. Impulsiveness was more Mason's style.

Not tonight.

This was too delicious an opportunity. "I'll need you to fix this for me—"

"I would think good and hard before you try to force me into anything inappropriate," she interrupted.

"Oh, I wouldn't do that." Kane let his deceptively soothing tone confuse her while he, too, slipped beneath the horse's neck to invade her safe spot. She stiffened even more.

Apparently she didn't like that at all…

Or did she? This close, he couldn't miss the uptick in her pulse at the base of her delicate throat or the way her tongue peeked out and slid slowly over her parted pink lips. He also caught the dip of her gaze to his fitted dress pants and button-down shirt before quickly returning to his face with a flash of guilt darkening her eyes.

Surely it wasn't terrible to use that interest to his every advantage? Selfish, maybe. He wouldn't let that sway him. "But I do think we will be getting to know each other very, very well."

"What?" The squeak in her voice and the hot blush that rushed into her cheeks told Kane he'd struck a nerve.

"Macarthur." He stepped closer, herding her toward the wall. "I recognize your name, Presley. Your stables, your family." He had a feeling his grin was not putting her at ease. "So does everyone else in the state, and beyond."

"So?"

Ah, he loved that breathless tone. "So, if we were together, it would put your seal of approval on Harrington stables."

"Together?"

Her voice was high and nervous. He propped one of his hands on the slatted wall above her shoulder. Had he reduced her to a one-word wonder? The thought made him grin even more. His proximity threw her off, and she seemed to squirm under his direct attention. And not in fear, which made the knowledge a delicious treat.

"Presumably together," he qualified. "As in, give the impression that we have a thing going." At her frown, he pushed farther. "Let everyone think we're lovers."

Suddenly, the beauty before him shut down. "Um, no."

"Are you sure about that?"

"I'm pretty sure I can think of another way to endorse your stables."

But that wasn't what he wanted. *Not anymore.* "Without sounding like you're being forced to?"

"Better than I could pretend to be your...ugh..."

"Lover?" Kane was getting the feeling that personal topics made Miss Macarthur very uncomfortable.

"Absolutely not."

Kane stepped back, palms out in a hands-off gesture. "Okay. We can simply tell them the real story instead. How your stepmother tried to swindle me out of an incredible amount of money—"

"She did not." Presley planted her fists on her hips, with the unintended effect of pulling her dress tighter over her body, giving him a glimpse of firm curves that set off interesting sparks in his brain.

Presley was oblivious. "She simply...well..."

"What?" Kane challenged, crossing his arms over his chest. "Made a mistake with a million-dollar horse that didn't belong to her?"

The expressions of indecision and ultimate acceptance that played out on Presley's face in that moment told Kane a hell of a lot about the woman before him. He knew plenty of men and women alike who would have thrown their hands up and declared the situation not of their making, so they weren't taking any responsibility. Not Presley. She could have thrown her stepmother to the fishes, but instead she tilted her chin and asked, "Exactly what expectations are we talking about here?"

Well, since he'd just thought this up on the fly, he wasn't sure. "We can discuss that."

"Now's as good a time as any." She moved to mimic his stance, crossing her arms beneath a surprisingly abundant chest.

He was beginning to see that this was a woman

of contradictions. Soft woman. Smart woman. Hard worker. Astute business manager. Timid on an interpersonal level. Which of these was the truest part of Presley Macarthur? The puzzle had his full attention, and it was the first time he'd been drawn away from his goals since—he didn't want to think about that.

"I already planned to spend a substantial amount of time making the social rounds over the next racing season," Kane said, softening his tone. He could afford to ease up when his instincts told him he was about to get what he wanted. "You could accompany me—"

"As in a date?"

He quickly suppressed a smirk. It wouldn't help to appear pompous. "Quite a few dates, actually. You can introduce me around, engage me in conversations that help showcase my business—"

"All while making you look like a stud yourself."

"If you underestimate the value of personal connections, you haven't been in this business long enough."

Despite being much younger than him—he'd guess almost ten years—he could see she understood. She knew how this industry operated. Potential customers wanted to work with people they knew, people who had already been vetted and accepted.

"We will attend together, and if I'm satisfied at the end of the season, all will be forgiven."

"No," she said, to his surprise, as she caught him in that narrow gaze once more. "Seems to me you'd be getting a lot of value for very little effort on your part."

"Is there something else you'd like me to…offer?"

"Yes. A ten percent discount on your refund."

Kane waited, almost amused at the vibration of energy holding her taut. What would that much emotion feel like? Taste like?

"Attending a bunch of events is going to cost me a good bit—of time *and* money. I think it's only fair to be compensated since you are the one getting the positive publicity."

Kane nodded slowly as he thought. He could afford to be generous at this point. "I think a consultation fee would be even more than that. Let's make it forty percent."

Those green eyes widened, which made Kane want to chuckle. Obviously she hadn't expected him to be so generous, but the facts were: he had more money than he knew what to do with and he wanted to spend more time with this woman. No matter what it cost him.

"But you will pretend to be my lover."

This time her protest was clear in her expression. He cut her off before she could speak. "No one is going to care about your endorsement if they know you've been paid to give one. And lovers touch. So this is part of the deal. Take it or leave it."

"Then one other condition," she said, holding her finger up in warning—as if that would ever hold him back. "You keep your hands to yourself."

"I'll keep my hands to myself, except when necessary."

"You mean when *you* think it's necessary?" Her disgusted tone told him just how she felt about his caveat.

She was a smart one. Considering the volatile extremes of this encounter, Kane wondered just how long that condition would last.

Or how long he'd be able to talk himself into obeying it. "But Presley, you are welcome to touch me any time you see fit."

"Since I'm being so generous," Kane said before Presley had a chance in hell of processing everything that had happened in the last half hour, "I propose we go into the house and get started."

"What?" Yeah, processing was not her strong suit at the moment. Which she didn't like. Being in control meant a lot to her.

"If you want to take Sun home tonight, there's no time like the present."

Why did his arrogant expression make her want to both smack him and rub the pad of her thumb along the arch of his raised eyebrow?

"Once we've made an appearance, I'll even make sure he gets properly loaded myself."

He gave her clothes a once-over. She'd come dressed to fit in with the party crowd, even though she had no intention of setting foot in the house. The irony wasn't lost on her. Kane thought he'd gained a sidekick who would give him an entrée into the tightest circles of racing society.

What would happen when he found out Presley was far from a social butterfly?

Large groups of people made her break out in hives. She'd only attended parties when her father insisted and usually spent the time doing her best wallflower impression. The men who constantly called her for advice and dropped by the stables to ask about their mares' latest ailments seemed to grow blinders the minute she slipped into a dress.

Not that she could blame them. Formal clothes looked bad on her and made her uncomfortable. Still, she was well enough known now that plenty of people would drop by her corner to talk business. But the endless conversations about horses dried up when prettier women entered the picture, making parties a minefield Presley had no ability or desire to navigate.

Maybe Kane wouldn't realize that until she had Sun safely home…

"Shall we?"

Kane graciously waved a hand to indicate she should precede him out of the stall. But Presley had now had an up-close encounter with the power and stubbornness behind the manners. They might have an agreement, but one look into his dark eyes told her he'd release the information about her stepmother and ruin her if she didn't cooperate.

A wolf tended to hide behind the good ol' boy facade here in the South.

She picked her way out of the stall, taking care not to dirty her sandals. The soothing cocoon of familiarity she always felt in the presence of animals immediately disappeared as she slipped into the wide alley that cut through the stables. As she passed Kane, she was once more impressed with his height; she barely reached his chest.

What little she knew of the Harrington brothers had

come from local gossip after they had taken over the manor, and then it had mostly covered Mason. Kane hadn't moved here full-time until very recently, and lived in his own home in the historic district downtown. According to the gossip mill, he had yet to hook up with anyone, but that wasn't for lack of trying on the ladies' parts. More than a few were eager to take Kane for a test drive.

Which meant Presley would not be their favorite person. Her steps slowed as she came back to the major flaw in his plan: she was not the best person to help Kane gain acceptance. And though she'd never admit it in a million years, the thought of this virile, astute man seeing just how inadequate she was in this situation had her cheeks burning already.

But she also couldn't let her reputation be ruined because of her stepmother's greed and ineptitude.

When she got close to the main door of the stables, Presley let her trepidation bring her to a full halt. Kane got a little ahead of her, then paused. He threw a look over his shoulder that seemed to ask what the problem was. How could he say so much with just a look? She had the feeling time spent with Kane Harrington would not be filled with idle chitchat.

Which would be a welcome prospect after endless hours of it with her stepmother.

Shoot! She'd forgotten her stepmother had spent all week expounding on what an event the Harrington's open house would be, which meant Marjorie would be a witness to this command performance. And she was a woman who was more than aware of Presley's faults and not shy about bringing them up when she had the chance. Not vindictively—it just never occurred to her flighty little self that what she was saying embarrassed Presley to no end.

Presley just couldn't do this. She'd end up falling flat on her face, literally and probably physically, too.

"What is it, Presley?"

If he had demanded, she might have lied. Instead his coaxing tone brought the most unexpected words to her lips. "How can I possibly pretend to be the—" she choked a little "—lover of a virtual stranger?"

Kane didn't seem the least bit fazed by her naive question. Instead he retraced his steps until he was all too close and her body was a jumble of sparks she didn't recognize.

"Would you like to practice first?" he asked, his husky tone sending a singular shiver down her spine.

Yes. "No! I just need time—"

"And I need everyone to talk about something else besides why the prize stud horse won't be making an appearance in my stables. The surest way to distract people from that is if we have a captive audience."

"That's what I'm worried about."

His unexpected chuckle had her stomach doing somersaults. What was wrong with her tonight?

Without warning, Kane brushed her chin with his long fingers. Startled at the warm contact, she glanced up, but the shadows over his face didn't give her any clues to his thoughts. He simply covered her lips with his.

Sensations immediately assaulted Presley, as if her

body weren't already on overload. This simple touch sent her over the top.

He didn't grope or force his tongue into her mouth. No, Kane wasn't an overeager boy looking for an easy in. Most of her experience had been like that. Instead, he rested against her mouth for a few moments. Just long enough for her to anticipate the next move.

When it came, it left her gasping. He brushed his lips lightly across hers, back and forth, until she opened to him. Still, he didn't force himself in. Instead he traced the outline of her lips with his tongue…and everything inside Presley tightened in response. One quick flick against her parted teeth, then he was gone.

Only then did Presley realize that her entire awareness had narrowed to the man touching her. The man she should have been scolding like a chaste maid from the seventeenth century. But no—

"How dare you?" she breathed.

He glanced down. Her gaze followed his and her cheeks started to burn.

Her hands clutched the lapels of his suit jacket, wrinkling the fabric. Her lungs strained for air as though she were a horse bellowing after a race. Her heart beat hard in her chest, the pounding of her pulse finding an embarrassing echo lower in her body.

And the man before her stood with his hands loose at his side, appearing completely unmoved.

Mortification that she could be overwhelmingly affected while he was completely cool hardened her attitude. "I told you to keep your hands to yourself."

"I wasn't using my hands," he said, holding them out to his sides. "See? No harm, no foul."

Despite herself, the deep tone of his voice gave her just a smidgen of satisfaction, even when he was lying through his teeth.

Three

"Sir, there's a trailer out—"

The words barely registering, Kane turned to find his stable manager, Jim Harvey, standing in the doorway of the barn. Jim's gaze moved from Kane's face to Presley.

His eyes widened.

"I'm so sorry to interrupt—"

"No problem," Kane cut him off quickly. He had a feeling Presley was on the edge of bolting at any moment. He needed this to be short and simple to set her at ease.

"Jim, this is Presley Macarthur."

Jim nodded. Recognition softened his expression, and he slipped off his cowboy hat. "Pleasure, ma'am."

He looked back and forth between the two of them,

obviously curious about what he'd walked in on but smart enough to know when something wasn't his business.

"Give us about an hour, if you don't mind," Kane went on, "then load Sun up for Miss Macarthur in the trailer so she can take him home."

Despite his confused look, Jim didn't question Kane in front of Presley. "Yes, sir." He turned to the woman who hadn't spoken a word. "I'll be right nearby, ma'am. We'll inspect the trailer when you get back."

"Thank you, Jim."

Ah, they were back to the confident, businesslike voice now. Probably for the best, though the off-guard squeaky one was Kane's favorite so far. What would she sound like if he kissed her again? Touched her more intimately? Cutting off the interesting train of thought, he offered Presley his arm and escorted her out of the stables.

They had barely stepped into the night air when she paused. "I don't understand. You're just gonna hand him back over to me?" She waved toward the brightly lit house. "Don't you want to test the goods before you make that decision?"

Kane couldn't help smirking. "I believe I already have."

Feeling the wave of shock shoot through her, he patted her hand in a benign gesture and continued on. As they crossed the drive back to the house, Kane found himself hyperaware of the woman at his side. The top of her head barely reached his shoulder, which made her taller than the average woman. She would fit right into the crook where his chest met his arm. The faint scent of honeysuckle teased his nose, an unusual perfume and one that reminded him of some of his happiest times on a horse in the countryside near his childhood home.

Honeysuckle had also grown on the edge of the yard at the house where he'd grown up before his mother died. He could still vividly remember her first attempts to teach him the gentle force needed to get the liquid from the honeysuckle flowers—and the tiny burst of sweetness on his tongue when he succeeded.

"Besides," he continued on, "I never go back on my word. Sun will be home tonight." They'd reached the covered side entry, and Kane paused with his hand on the doorknob. "This situation is tricky, but I know you'll do what's best for your family and your business."

Blackmail wasn't a sexy subject, but before they stepped onto the stage, Kane wanted Presley to remember exactly what was at stake here. The stiffness of her body told him more about her state of mind than her simple nod of acquiescence.

He ushered her inside with a hand at the small of her back, and the lights from the Swarovski crystal chandeliers left her blinking. In fact, her whole demeanor changed the minute they walked through the door. If someone had told him a person could become invisible, he wouldn't have believed them—until he saw Presley practically pull off the impossible.

They'd barely made it halfway down the back breezeway when Mason and EvaMarie stepped out of the office. "Kane," his brother called.

Only as he stopped and registered the concern on Mason's face did Kane remember that he hadn't taken the time to shut down his computer before storming out the door. The knowledge sat between them like a lead brick. Mason knew exactly what that email from Vanessa Gentry would have done to Kane—he'd been there when Emily had left him behind, and watched as Kane systematically let everything disappear from his life except their shared goal.

Because life was easier that way.

Hoping to ward off any questions from his impulsive sibling, Kane preempted the conversation. "Mason, this is Presley Macarthur."

His brother blinked, then focused on the woman on Kane's arm. "Oh, from Macarthur Haven?"

Presley's hand tightened on Kane's elbow. But she relaxed a touch when EvaMarie nodded and smiled. "Hello, Presley."

"Congratulations, EvaMarie."

The lovely woman, who had been Mason's first love and had been the epitome of a woman defeated by life when they'd returned to Kentucky, now practically glowed. "Thank you."

As the women chatted for a moment about the engagement, Mason looked at Kane with a raised brow.

"There's been a change of plans," Kane murmured, keeping his voice low though he'd moved slightly away from Presley.

"As in?"

Kane turned to face his brother. "It appears Ms. Macarthur didn't have the proper authority to sell Sun."

Mason cursed. "That's a helluva mistake to make."

An understatement if ever there was one. But then,

Kane was being generous when he labeled Marjorie Macarthur's actions a *mistake*.

"What are we gonna do now? Our plan going forward hinged on having a celebrated stud for the stables." Mason's worry practically vibrated in his voice.

"Never fear," Kane assured him, as he had many times in the last two years. They'd been through a lifetime of ups and downs together. Kane wasn't about to let them fail. "I've got a new plan that will work just fine."

His brother's gaze followed him as he turned back to the women and slipped his arm around Presley's shoulders. The muscles beneath his palm tightened and her smile faltered for a moment, but he didn't move away. The sooner she became used to his touch, the better.

The more he touched her tonight, the sooner word would start to spread. Nothing overtly sexual. He'd keep it completely casual—not that anyone would interpret it that way.

Kane wanted his name linked with hers from this moment forward…for however long this situation remained beneficial to them both.

Mason continued to watch him with interest and just a touch of shock. Not surprising, since Kane hadn't been publicly involved with a woman since Emily left.

He hadn't wanted to be and was actually shocked by how much he wanted it now. But then he spotted Presley's stepmother over Mason's shoulder. When her stepdaughter's presence registered, Ms. Macarthur trotted their way with the grace of an overadorned poodle, and Kane had only a moment to wonder if he really knew what he'd gotten himself into.

Her loud greeting only confirmed it. "Lordy, Presley! Is that really hay in your hair?"

As her stepmother's words echoed throughout the long, open back hall of the Harrisons' home, Presley wished she could sink into the floor.

Not that embarrassing her was anything new for Marjorie. No, it actually seemed to be her regular pastime. But repeated experience didn't take away the sinking feeling in Presley's stomach or the hot flush that flooded her cheeks so quickly that she was surprised she didn't pass out from blood loss.

Her stepmother practically shoved herself between Presley and Kane. "Look at you. Hay on your dress, dirt on your sandals. What were you doing out in the barn, you silly girl?"

"I think the answer to that might be just as embarrassing as the question."

With that single answer, Kane caught the attention of everyone within hearing distance. Presley wished she could fade into the flowered wallpaper as his laser gaze inspected her from head to toe, no doubt noticing her lack of style and ability to attract dirt no matter how hard she tried to stay clean. But he didn't mention it. Oh, no. Kane had embraced this pretend relationship wholeheartedly.

If he only knew what a mistake he was making—though it was beneficial for her that he didn't. The sooner he realized she wasn't going to be the perfect princess on his arm at all these events, the sooner she'd have to repay him in full.

"Sorry, sweetheart," he murmured near her ear, though his voice still seemed to carry. "I didn't mean to get you all dirty."

Holy Moses. The heat that swept through her as she heard him talk should have been an embarrassment. She should have been wishing he would quit making a spectacle of her. Instead, she wished he would keep on talking and make her forget about their audience.

He reached out to snag the small piece of hay from the tip of her loose ponytail—the only hairstyle she could comfortably create—and then held it up as he smiled into her eyes. There was mischief in that look, and also something deeper, darker, that tempted her to join him in his game.

Only she'd never learned how to play.

Her stepmother was just as nonplussed, which was the first time Presley had ever seen that happen. Marjorie watched Kane's actions with a kind of wide-eyed fascination, then glanced back and forth between the two of them as confusion clouded her expression.

Finally she focused solely on Presley, frowning. "Well, you should have at least told me you had a date. I could have helped you find something more appropriate to wear."

Apparently the embarrassment wasn't going to end any time soon. Over Marjorie's shoulder Presley could see a group of women—the same debutantes who had haunted her existence since she was about fourteen—whispering furiously and grinning. All except one: Joan Everly. She simply stared through narrowed lids, anger slowly taking over her polite society mask.

"Oh," Kane said, his amused tone warning Presley she wouldn't like what was coming. "I think her dress suited *my* purposes just fine."

Judging from the few gasps she heard out of the debs, Kane's voice had carried. But Presley could sense the disbelief in people's reactions. And now she was done being put on display.

She turned around and blindly grasped the nearest door handle and pushed her way through. She didn't care where she went, as long as it was away from prying eyes. But the shuffle of feet and the click of dress shoes on the floor behind her told her she hadn't escaped. She had company. Great. More confrontation was just what she wanted right now.

Give her a stubborn horse or an uppity ranch hand and she met the challenge like a trouper. Social settings and public displays of anything, much less affection, were definitely not her forte.

A familiar weariness seeped into her muscles. The feeling had made its first appearance as soon as her father's funeral was over and all the guests were gone. Since then it returned regularly, but she always pushed it back. She didn't have time to be tired, especially not with the task of taking care of her stepmother on top of her already heavy schedule managing the business.

So just as she had a hundred times in the past six months, she pushed the gray cloud back and straightened her spine. When she spun around, she saw that only their small group had followed, but it was Marjorie who spoke first.

"Presley, what is going on here?"

Confusion still reigned in Marjorie's expression, but years of being ridiculed for not living up to Marjorie's expectations, not being feminine enough, being too smart and serious all the time…none of that made Presley want to confide exactly what had happened in the barn earlier. Her tongue stuck to the roof of her mouth. How in the world could she possibly say out loud that the only way she could attract a man of Kane's caliber was because her stepmother had tried to swindle the Harringtons out of a large amount of money?

Of course, given the result, Marjorie would probably see that as doing a good deed.

To Presley's surprise, Kane spoke up. "The fact is, Presley wouldn't even be here without your criminal lack of judgment, Ms. Macarthur."

Shock rippled through the room, settling in Presley's core. No one had ever stood up for her. Not even her daddy. When he'd brought Marjorie into their lives, he'd hoped that she'd teach his daughter to be a woman. Marjorie's abject failure in that area was considered all Presley's fault. And though he had loved her, her father hadn't hidden his disappointment from her.

The look of shock on Mason's face was priceless. Especially when Kane stepped closer to Presley and draped his arm around her shoulders again. But Kane ignored his brother as he said, "Oh, don't get me wrong. I'm very grateful she did show up."

Marjorie wasn't buying it. "If you expect me to believe that my Presley snared the catch of the county in thirty minutes, in that dress, you must think I'm really stupid."

Presley wasn't sure what set off her normally dormant outrage. The stress of the day. Kane's blackmail. Or everyone's obvious disbelief even as Kane insisted they were interested in each other. *If you had to sell it that hard, might as well not sell it at all.*

Without thought Presley stomped forward, invading her stepmother's personal space. "What I think is that you couldn't care less how your actions affect me or anyone else who has to put up with your antics."

"Well, I knew that my very smart stepdaughter would smooth everything out," Marjorie whined.

"Excuse me?" Suddenly all the tension and upset of the night became too much and Presley was the one who couldn't control her voice. She made a desperate attempt to contain the words but couldn't keep them back. "You bargained with an animal you knew didn't belong to you, but that's okay because Presley will figure it all out?"

Marjorie blanched. "I know you love the horse, but money is—"

Presley stepped uncomfortably close, lowering her voice. "Not something you have an unlimited amount of anymore. And if you ever pull a stunt like this again, I'll do everything in my power to have Grant break Father's will. Do you understand me?"

"He couldn't."

"He's a great lawyer. I'm sure he could manage it for me."

Something in her expression must have scared Marjorie, because she focused on Presley's face and remained silent for a long moment. Finally she gave a stiff nod, then blinked, and the flighty society lady was back in action. "No need to be so serious, dear. This is a fun night. For you more than most, am I right?"

It was no use. All the anger and frustration flooding Presley's veins had nowhere to go, no way out. Some days she thought running around in endless circles with her stepmother would never end. Why her father had subjected her to this particular hell, she'd never know.

And despite the threat she'd just made, she had little expectation of any change. The next shiny diamond to cross Marjorie's path would catch her attention and block out all reason.

Leaving Presley with another six-foot-four-inch problem to solve—a magnitude totally out of her league.

Kane's response didn't exactly put her fears to rest. "I assure you, Ms. Macarthur, Presley and I have gotten off to a very good start. And we will be seeing a great deal of each other in the future."

His words should have heaped another helping onto her pile of worry. Instead anticipation tingled in her stomach, warming her from the inside out. This was wrong. All wrong.

Presley preferred situations she could control.

"That settles that, then," her stepmother offered with a toothy grin.

Marjorie's problems always disappeared. Presley's merely grew. And she had a feeling she was way out of her depth on this one.

Four

Kane wasn't sure he was surprised when the woman who answered the Macarthurs' front door told him, "Miss Presley is almost always in the barn." The Presley he'd met the night before certainly wasn't a Miss Kentucky pageant type. But he had to admit he didn't have a lot of experience with daughters of bigwigs who were willing to get their hands dirty.

He was used to the daughters of fellow laborers, who loved animals and worked just as hard as any of the men.

He certainly hadn't expected to hear Presley's raised voice as he closed the stable door behind him. Several hands at the far end of the aisle kept their heads down and focused intently on their work, pointedly ignoring the noise. A lone man stood in the aisle closer to

Kane, stance rigid, arms crossed over his chest, gaze trained tightly on the open stall in front of him until Kane walked into his peripheral vision.

Their eyes met as Presley's hardened voice continued to boom out from inside a nearby stall. She was scolding someone Kane couldn't see. "I realize she doesn't like her hooves cleaned. First of all, if you can't work around that, you aren't good enough or experienced enough to be employed here. Second of all, if you ever lay a hand on any of my horses like that again, it's the last horse you'll touch in this barn. Do I make myself clear?"

There was a silence, and Kane saw the man in front of him tense up even more, if that was possible. From within the stall, the employee being reprimanded replied with a tight "yes, ma'am."

Then Kane's companion in the aisle relaxed.

"Now," Presley said, her voice turning indulgent as though she was trying to teach something to a particularly hardheaded child, "I'll do one hoof for you, then you can do the others while I watch."

No argument was forthcoming. Kane grinned, imagining the grown stable hand being taken back to Hoof Cleaning 101 and the ribbing he would get from his coworkers later today. Sounded like he deserved it, though.

The man who stood before Kane in the aisle finally held a hand out to him. "Hello there. I'm Bennett, the Macarthurs' stable manager."

Kane shook, introducing himself in turn. He jerked his head in the direction of the stall. "Shouldn't you be dealing with that?"

Bennett shrugged. "Usually I do, but Miss Presley is a very hands-on owner. Has been since her daddy first brought her into the stables." He turned his gaze back to the stall door as if checking progress. "There are certain things she will always handle herself. Mistreatment, no matter how small, is something she's adamant about being informed of immediately. We have a zero-tolerance policy here."

"But she didn't throw him out on his ass at the first sign?"

"Depends on what happens. She's also a fair employer. She understands that many of these men have families to support or are just learning their trade." Bennett's craggy face softened with approval. "The men know it, too. They don't cross her. We rarely have problems, but she's quick to handle whatever comes along."

So she had experience along with her degree in equine management. No wonder she was well respected. Kane had done a little digging before showing up this morning, just to double-check the information he'd gathered from the grapevine. But he hadn't just been after her business credentials—EvaMarie had known a lot more about Presley personally, piquing Kane's interest on a totally different topic.

Her reluctance to make personal appearances at parties had been well noted throughout the years, often leaving her open to ridicule from other women in their social circle. While her business reputation had been solid long before her father's death, her social reputation had often floundered. After watching Presley for those few moments with Marjorie the night before, he could easily guess why.

She'd never been allowed to find her true footing. To be herself in the face of peer pressure from society's little darlings. Kane's sudden desire to help her set off alarm bells in his head. The last thing he should do was attempt to fix anyone. He'd been down that road before, and he simply wasn't built for it.

It was the only thing he'd ever failed at in his life.

But Presley was a whole different ball game from Emily. The last thing she needed was taking care of—as her management skills attested. If Kane could help her tweak her public persona while they were together, it would simply be an added bonus of their arrangement. He was way more interested in what would happen in private when their time in the spotlight was done.

"See, you just have to know how to handle her. Now go help Arden get the water tank fixed," he heard Presley command.

Something about her confidence made Kane smile— and his body come to attention. Presley wouldn't be a limp, lazy princess who expected someone to make her happy in bed. Oh, no, this woman would be a full participant.

Not that he should be considering that so soon…

As a shamefaced man came out the stall door with his thumbs hooked in his jeans pockets, Bennett directed him down the aisle with a jerk of his head. He glanced as Kane. "That could have ended very badly, with fussin' and fightin'. But not with Miss Presley. Somehow she can take 'em to task, put 'em on the right path and get everyone movin' forward without a knock-down-drag-out." He winked. "But I'm always nearby, just in case."

Bennett followed his employee down the aisle, leaving Kane to approach the stall door all alone.

Presley's murmured words to the mare soothed Kane's nerves, which he now realized had been standing at attention from the first moment he'd heard her raised voice. Unfortunately, the sight of her as she bent over and carefully inspected each of the horse's hooves had other things coming to attention, too.

Last night, Presley's flowy dress had been hiding some serious curves. Today she wore a very soft-looking T-shirt tucked into a pair of jeans. Rounded hips blossomed from a tiny waist hugged by denim. When she stood to pat the horse's back, he saw that the cotton of her shirt clung just as faithfully in all the right places.

Holy hell. He was in trouble…so why was he grinning like an idiot?

He forced his gaze upward, only to encounter a glare directed his way. Funny, it didn't dampen his excitement. "Hello, Presley."

"What are you doing here?" she asked, narrowing her gaze on him.

"Watching you in action," he replied, fully understanding how much that would aggravate her. "I'm impressed."

To his surprise, she had quite a sarcastic mouth on her. "I'm so glad you liked what you saw."

But her bravado didn't stop a flush spreading over her cheeks. Perhaps as a gentleman, he should clarify his previous comment. "There's a difference between appreciating a woman and disrespecting her—my mama taught me that."

"So you're respectfully blackmailing me?"

"Considering the concessions I've made, isn't it more of a mutual agreement than blackmail?"

"An agreement I'm forced to enter into if I don't want my family and business reputation ruined… I think that does qualify as blackmail."

That bossy tone should not be so arousing. And he couldn't deny her logic. "Maybe I wanted to spend time with you."

"A woman you didn't know?" She scoffed. "You'd be the first."

With just those few words, she confirmed EvaMarie's story from this morning. Kane kept silent.

Sticking to his stance might take away his gentleman card, but he wouldn't miss what was coming for the world.

Presley skirted around the horse's rump, making her way to a clipboard on top of a cupboard by the door. "Most men are only hoping for one thing when they spend time with me," she said, studying the papers with unnecessary intensity. "My expertise with horses."

Kane nodded, even though she pretended she wasn't watching him. But he saw the quick sideways glance, no matter how brief.

She continued, "Not frilly dresses and small talk."

Deciding she'd had enough time to spout nonsense, he crossed the threshold of the stall. To her credit, she didn't retreat as he neared. He didn't box her in but got close enough that he could smell her shampoo. "There are things a lot sexier than social niceties."

It was too soon, but he couldn't stop himself from reaching out to sample some of the thick blond strands of hair in her ponytail. Silky—just as he'd imagined.

"Why are you touching me?" she asked.

Her tone wasn't quite as breathless as he'd have liked. He sensed just a hint of excitement.

"You're right," he murmured. "I'm sorry. I'm simply fascinated by the color, texture."

She smoothed her hands over her hair. "I don't know if I can do this."

That's what her mouth said, but as soon as he looked up to catch her eyes, she glanced away. Avoidance. At least it confirmed what he suspected was happening here. Time for a different approach: honesty. "Look, Presley. I know that this might be uncomfortable. I'm simply trying to make things more natural between us."

"I don't think I like it."

"But you aren't sure?"

She stiffened, her look transforming into a glare. "That's incredibly sexist."

"Or incredibly honest." He pushed on, leaving the inference of his own interest behind for the moment. There was another way to get her riled up, which he enjoyed far too much. "I told you, touching is expected. Would you rather we practice in public?"

"I'd rather not practice at all."

"But practice makes perfect. Besides, I find I enjoy touching you. It's okay if you like it, too. It doesn't have to go any further than, well, public displays of affection."

Presley opened her mouth to speak, then paused. She studied him for a moment, but he had the feeling she wasn't really looking at him. "Why do I feel like we've covered this before?"

He let his amusement mold his mouth...just a little. "Guess it's something we'll have to keep doing until we get it right between us."

Her perfect bow-shaped lips twitched, lush in their natural state. He could swear she was holding in laughter. "Like, practice?"

"Maybe."

Her entire face opened up, letting her enjoyment of the moment shine through her earlier irritation. Seeing Presley give in to her amusement was sexy as hell. Her smile was wide and unself-conscious, her eyes bright and seeking his. When he laughed with her, the glow increased like a power surge.

Gorgeous.

A noise interrupted them. Kane turned to see Bennett in the doorway. Presley's laughter shut off instantly.

"Miss Presley, Sun is ready."

Kane watched from the corner of his eye as she nodded. Bennett left, but Presley continued to stare at the doorway. She shifted. She swallowed. Kane waited her out.

"Was there something you needed, Kane?" she finally asked.

Did she worry about him being too close to the stud? "I did want to speak with you. Iron out a few details."

"Well, I have things I need to do right now."

As if that would stop him. "I don't mind tagging along."

From the look on her face, Kane could tell she wasn't sure what to feel. Ah, he was making progress...

Presley preceded Kane down the barn corridor, feeling flustered. Why in the world hadn't she told him to hit the road? She should have. After all, the man was completely taking advantage of a situation she had no control over.

But she couldn't forget the look in his eyes when she'd first spotted him in the doorway. He could have leered. He could have been indifferent. But the pure male appreciation wasn't something she'd encountered before today. Oh, men had told her she was pretty, though it never rang true. But something about Kane's gaze, unsullied by greed or arrogance, was special.

Maybe that was why she hadn't fought this harebrained scheme harder. Maybe she was more than a little interested to see exactly how this would all go. There was probably something very wrong with that line of thinking, but Presley was nothing if not honest with herself.

When they got to Sun's stall, Kane didn't force his way in or try to take over. She'd come across a lot of men who thought they knew better than a woman in the stables...until she taught them they were wrong. It didn't take a huge confrontation or butting of heads. She simply let them go on until they ran out of steam, then stepped in and quietly set them straight.

Unless she needed to raise her voice. Then she did.

Nodding to Bennett, who was already in the stall, Presley put her hand on Sun's withers and whispered near the horse's ear. He whipped his head around fast, and Presley heard Kane's step behind her, but she didn't flinch. They'd played this game before, her and Sun. The horse didn't bite or hit her with his heavy head. Instead he corrected at the last minute and pressed the side of his muzzle against her shoulder, pushing hard. She stumbled, chuckling, then reached up to give him a rough rub behind his ears.

"Likes to play, does he?" Kane asked.

Bennett laughed from his position on Sun's other side. "Believe it or not, he's like a big kid. And she's incredible with him."

Presley felt warmth creep into the pit of her stomach. No matter how often someone complimented her on her knowledge, it was this connection with the animals in her care that meant the most to her. Especially with Sun.

She checked him over quickly, just to make sure in the daylight that there were no adverse effects from last night's quick trip. Then she and Bennett discussed what he needed over the next week. Her big baby got a good rubbing and a piece of apple she was hiding in her pocket before they left.

After locking Sun back down, Bennett said goodbye to them outside the stud's stall door and went to tend to the other horses.

"He's right, you know," Kane said, "I've never seen anyone so in tune with horses."

Presley ducked her head, embarrassed by Kane's

compliment, even while that warm glow spread. "They can be sensitive creatures. It's all about knowing them, what they need. Of course, Sun and I go way back." Maybe that's why the horse was the one thing her daddy had willed to her alone. "Daddy bought him for me the year my mother died," she found herself adding.

Wow, what a maudlin subject to introduce. But Kane didn't hesitate before he asked, "How old?"

Though she now regretted bringing it up, she answered, "Six."

"I was fifteen when my mother died after a long fight with cancer."

She glanced at him in surprise. Somewhere in the back of her mind, she might have remembered this about the Harrington family but had forgotten in the loads of other, more recent, gossip. His dark eyes were solemn, his gaze direct. It almost made her feel as though she could actually talk to him about things—private things she mostly kept to herself now that her daddy was gone.

"Did your father also insist on bringing in a new mommy?" she murmured, though she did add a bit of a smirk to lighten the impact of her question.

Kane smiled too, but his dark gaze remained serious. "Nope. From then on out, it was just us guys. Action movies and baseball games. When we were older, beer and pizza nights."

"That must have been nice…"

"What must have been nice?" Marjorie's voice was jarring, not just because it was so close and loud, but because Presley could only remember one other time her stepmother had ventured into the stables. She'd never been back.

Presley quickly closed her gaping mouth as Marjorie appeared from behind Kane.

Kane didn't flinch, of course. "We were just talking about remarrying."

"I see," Marjorie said, nodding as if she had all the knowledge in the world. Her bejeweled pantsuit and heels were completely out of place in her surroundings. "I'm afraid our girl has never appreciated what her father and I tried to do for her. I'm sure you were more grateful to your father..."

"He never remarried."

Short and sweet. No apologies. Presley was beginning to enjoy this.

The shocked look on Marjorie's face melted into confusion, but she quickly recovered. Presley suppressed a sigh as her stepmother prattled on about her own marriage and how she couldn't understand why Presley had never taken to her. *There ya go. Tell all our dirty little secrets.*

"Did you need something, Marjorie?" Presley finally cut in.

"Oh." Marjorie blinked, obviously reorienting herself to her mission. "I saw you arrive, Kane, and wanted to make sure there were no hard feelings from last night."

No *I'm sorry for stealing your money.* But why would Marjorie think she needed to apologize for that?

"I'm over the moon to have my Presley taking care of things and wouldn't want you to think otherwise," Marjorie said. "She keeps this place running..."

Presley raised a single brow, surprised Marjorie tore herself away from her society lunches long enough to notice, much less be grateful.

"If I could just get her to listen to me more—"

Please, stop talking.

But no, Marjorie just had to keep going. "She has so much potential, you know."

"And she's living up to it every day," Kane replied.

Marjorie and Presley both focused in on Kane. Presley couldn't tell which of them was more shocked. No one had ever defended her against Marjorie's inane yet often hurtful prattle in this house. Her father had let it go on and never gave a clue to his own thoughts. At times, he had even reiterated Marjorie's message in his own way.

Oh, he'd loved Presley. She had no doubt. But he'd thought she'd be better off as a prissy princess, not a tomboy, even though she could run this business better than any man here. She'd never understood that.

Kane broke into her thoughts. "Now if you'll excuse us, we have a lunch date."

What? she almost asked, but Kane's steady gaze kept her mouth shut. Presley gave a short nod. Anything to get her away from Marjorie and this uncomfortable conversation.

"Surely not dressed like that?" Marjorie asked, eyeing Presley's dusty jeans and T-shirt.

Presley glanced over to find Kane doing the same, with a far different look in his eyes than she expected. "Why not?" he asked, his voice just a touch husky. "Love the jeans, hon."

That wink would have made any woman swoon. Presley recognized it as a weapon against her normally strong defenses. How long could she hold out against all this Harrington appeal?

Five

Presley soon realized that Kane wasn't kidding. He nodded when she said she wanted to wash up, but he encouraged her not to change—the restaurant wouldn't care.

What kind of restaurant was that? Surely the world's newest billionaire wasn't taking her out for fast food? She did at least upgrade from a dusty shirt to a clean one with a Wonder Woman logo. Both out of defiance and a deep-down desire for Kane to see the real her. The girl who couldn't care less about society chatter but enjoyed action movies and riding and comic books.

Eventually it would bore him and he'd leave her alone, especially if he had to take the real her out in public, right?

The quicker disillusionment set in, the quicker she'd be free of this dang bargain.

When she rejoined him at the front of the house, he glanced down at the front of her shirt and grinned but didn't say anything. She wasn't sure exactly what his reaction meant. He led her to a dark burgundy luxury SUV and let her in the passenger side like a true gentleman. As she waited for him to join her, she took a deep breath. The inside of the vehicle smelled of new leather seats and the cologne Kane had been wearing the night before. As he opened the door, she breathed again.

Boy, did he smell good. She probably still smelled like the barn. Now she wondered if she should have changed into a dress, but then she would have been completely uncomfortable and self-conscious. As if she wasn't self-conscious now—

"Let's just relax and get to know each other, okay?" Kane asked, interrupting the momentum of her thoughts.

Her nod was a little jagged. In the barn, she'd been fine. Not totally in control, but confident in her surroundings. Now she didn't have that, and the need to second-guess everything meant she'd be on edge the entire time.

Just let it go.

"You should feel lucky," she blurted out as he turned around in the wide drive.

"How's that?" he asked, flashing her a grin that took at least half a dozen years off his features. Kane was often solemn-looking. *Why was that?*

"Marjorie hasn't been in the barn in a long time. Years, I think. But she made a special trip just to see you."

To her amusement, his brows shot up. "I don't know if I'd call either of us lucky for that."

Laughing with him felt good. She hadn't done that with many people since her father died. He'd been one of the few who actually got her off-the-wall sense of humor. She missed that feeling of communal amusement.

Kane directed the conversation back to horses as they drove through the heart of town and out the other side. The west end of town was just as rural as the east, but the farms were smaller. Usually the families over here raised cattle or did specialty farming on a more modest scale than the elite horse farms on the east. There was also a small community college out this way that Presley had only visited a time or two for concerts.

Kane drove with confident ease. His hands on the wheel were things of masculine beauty. She could watch his sure grip and the slide of his palm against the leather all day. To her surprise, he shared some of what he and his brother were planning to do with their own farm.

When he suddenly pulled into a lot and parked, Presley glanced around, having been distracted by their debate over different animal supplement techniques. The gravel lot was a tiny triangle at the intersection of two roads. There were only a few vehicles besides theirs. Several people had congregated on the tiny outdoor porch of the restaurant at the widest point of the lot.

"Um, I haven't been here before," she said, studying the place with a bit of skepticism.

In Kentucky, it wasn't a stretch to say some of the best food came from some of the most run-down-look-

ing joints. Her daddy had often picked up food for her
from restaurants like this when they traveled. One of
his protective measures had been to bring it back to the
hotel. He never let her go to a part of town he didn't feel
was safe for her. But this place was in her own back-
yard, and she'd never heard of it.

Guess her high-class snobbery was showing.

"We'd better get in line," Kane advised. "We've got
about ten minutes before this place is packed."

Um, okay.

The main wing of the two-story building was small,
with a weathered, pointed roof. A square addition had
been fitted against the back to form a stubby L shape.
While relatively clean, the place showed a lot of wear.
"What kind of food is it?" she asked as they crossed
the lot.

Eyeing the casual attire of those already lined up, she
realized Kane had been right. No need to worry about
her barn clothes here.

"They have some different things, but the main fare
is southern-style barbecue," Kane said with obvious
enthusiasm. "I've been eating here since I was about
ten years old."

Well, if this restaurant had been around that long,
they must be serving something good. And the cuisine
explained some of the grubbiness—the barbecue smoke
had been building up for a long time.

Kane grew quiet while they waited, but it wasn't an
uncomfortable silence. He pointed out a menu on the
wall so she could get a preview. Then he held his tongue
until the door opened and they followed the small crowd

to the hostessing stand, if one could call it that. The timber walls were covered with handwritten messages left by numerous patrons. Quarters were close, and the line behind them promised to make things even cozier.

But they shouldn't have trouble getting a table, if the hostess's big grin and hug for Kane were any indication. He and the older woman chatted a few minutes, getting caught up. "The usual spot?" she asked, her gaze flicking curiously to Presley and back.

Kane nodded, and the hostess handed menus and wrapped silverware off to a younger waitress without a word. Kane gestured for Presley to follow the woman, his firm hand at the base of her spine leaving her all too aware of him as she contemplated the very tight spiral staircase they had to climb.

"Hope I don't meet anyone on their way down," she joked.

There truly was only space for one-way traffic. "That's how you get to know your neighbors," Kane deadpanned.

Yeah, this man would surely get her sense of humor.

The stairs opened onto a narrow aisle on the second floor lined with rustic booths. The slanted roof lent an interesting angle to the ceiling, and one side of the floor looked out over the room and bar below. The waitress seated them in the far corner in front of a triangular window that fit into the angles of the room.

As she took her seat across from him, Presley caught Kane watching her. He didn't speak, but somehow she knew he was wondering what she thought. Country music cranked up from the jukebox downstairs. Presley grinned. "This is interesting." Like some of the honky-tonks she'd heard the stable hands talk about but had never gone to herself.

Kane nodded. "I love things with character. This place has it in spades. Just wait until you taste the food."

He didn't try to direct her in what she should eat. Instead he waited while she read every inch of the menu.

"Anything especially good?" she asked.

Kane shrugged. "Over the years I've had just about everything. But the ribs are my favorite. Oh, and the mac and cheese." He nodded slowly as if he were a wise sage imparting an eternal truth.

Presley smothered a grin and went back to her menu. Kane didn't even crack his.

"This is where we had all of our fancy dinners growing up," Kane said almost absently. "My dad loved it here."

Presley couldn't help but compare the worn decor and friendly atmosphere with the stuffy yet impressive restaurants where she'd been forced to celebrate her birthdays over the years. "Things must feel a lot different now." After all, Kane could probably buy this place fifty times over if he wanted.

He focused in on her for a moment, the intensity of his look causing her to catch her breath. "Some things haven't changed at all."

Before she could even question his statement in her own mind, their waitress returned to take their order. Anxious to revisit her own barbecue memories with her father, she chose the one food Marjorie would have thoroughly admonished her for eating in public: ribs.

Though she ordered hers with a milder sauce than what Kane was having.

Her simple decision made Presley want to smile. She was a grown woman and didn't need anyone's permission for the choices she made. Being with Kane made her want to explore a different side of herself. Maybe it was his open acknowledgment of Marjorie's lack of parenting skills. Maybe it was the teasing or casual use of sexual innuendos. Something about Kane made her want to take pleasure in life instead of being all business for a change.

"I figured you'd want more definitive details about our agreement since you're a businesswoman," Kane said.

Heat swept over her skin. Apparently she was the only one ready to leave business behind. How embarrassing. After all, a man like Kane would certainly not be interested in a real date with a woman like her.

"Right. Yes, I would," she managed.

She'd gotten lost in the personal conversation and forgotten that she was only here for business. Kane just preferred to conduct his business over barbecue rather than at Pierre's downtown.

Presley tried to push the discouraging thoughts away and focus on what Kane was telling her.

"It occurred to me, after I was able to give this arrangement more thought last night," he said, his face once more solemn, without a hint of his earlier wink, "there might be another way to work off your family's debt."

For a moment, Presley was paralyzed all the way

to her core. She wasn't sure if she was worried he was about to disrespect her or if she was worried he was about to give her a way out. Which was wrong, but somehow she couldn't help it. She couldn't stop herself from wondering if he'd spent all night trying to find a way out of spending so much time with her.

"You mean my stepmother's debt?" she said, wincing at the slight croak in her voice.

No matter how he'd grown up, Kane couldn't have looked more regal than when he gave her a single, solemn nod. "There might be another way to preserve her reputation—and mine."

Presley narrowed her gaze on him. This little meeting had taken on a completely different tone with just a few words. "I'm listening."

"You can keep the money I paid you for stud service."

Her eyes widened as her dirty little mind went in a totally different direction than it should have. "Excuse me?"

"For Sun."

Of course. He wouldn't have meant anything else. And if it had been anyone else speaking, that was the first thing she'd have thought. But this was Kane Harrington. And somehow, in the past twenty-four hours, Presley had gone from viewing this as a business arrangement to wishing for something Kane probably wouldn't enjoy as much—kiss or no kiss.

Before she could do something stupid, like voice her disappointment, their waitress set two steaming platters on the table between them. Presley looked down at the juicy half rack of ribs and wondered what the hell she'd been thinking. Surely she'd make a complete mess out of this. The way she had of her personal perceptions about what was happening here.

Just as her worries escalated, her hands trembling with that unmistakable performance anxiety she often suffered in social situations, Presley took a deep breath and forced herself to stop and focus on the business at hand.

Business. It was only business, and that she knew how to handle. *That's all it ever could be, right?*

Presley forgot about the food between them. "How much?"

Kane's impassive expression wasn't giving much away. "I've got the paperwork in the SUV. You can invoice out every use of Sun for stud, and we will subtract the normal fee from your balance. If at any time this arrangement no longer suits you, just pay the balance in full and we're done."

"And you again have free rein to ruin my reputation?" she asked, not buying this simple fix. At all.

"As you'll learn, I always do what is required. But in this case, I don't think that will be necessary. Do you?"

Kane relaxed into the worn leather-upholstered booth, watching Presley carefully pick her way through the ribs on her plate. She tried so hard to be neat, to not make a mess. He expected her to break out a fork at any minute.

He'd figured the business discussion would put a damper on what was happening between them, but the matter had needed to be addressed. Kane had always been a fan of getting the necessary ugly stuff out of the way first.

Presley had gone from the comfortable and confident woman who had climbed into his SUV with a mild sense of rebellion, wearing jeans and a T-shirt, to self-conscious and stiff the minute he'd brought up their arrangement. He'd been able to see the transformation in her expression, the way she held herself.

The dichotomy fascinated him, kept him on the edge of his seat in a way few things had lately.

"We can start small on the social scale. Practice, if you will." He flashed a small grin even though she'd gone stock-still. "A small party shooting pool in the basement at my house tonight. You didn't get to see the entertainment area downstairs, did you?"

Presley was still holding two rib bones in her fingertips. Was she ever going to just eat? Despite her surprise, she wasn't just accepting his request.

"What if I have plans for tonight?" she asked.

Like she could fool him. "Do you?"

She frowned. Had she really thought he wouldn't challenge that?

"No, but—"

"Good. You can be there about eight. It'll just be a few people."

She didn't move. Didn't agree. And it didn't matter—he wasn't giving her the chance to back out.

"And by the way, if there should be any side effects to our spending time together—"

"Side effects?" That squeak reminded him of their

first encounter, which had only been last night. They'd packed that short time full of interesting things, hadn't they?

Kane didn't repeat himself. Instead he gave her a direct look, letting her see his intent front and center.

Kane loved to challenge her, just to watch her think. Her expression only hinted at what was happening inside, but he could tell she was trying to figure out how to handle him.

"Anything that happens will be by mutual consent." Now she had his word.

"Aren't you gonna dig in?" he asked.

Presley blinked. Then he nodded at her plate, and she glanced down at her fingers. She was still gripping the bones as if it was the only sure move she knew.

"Like this," he said, then tore several ribs off his rack and lifted them to his mouth, biting into them unceremoniously with a mock growl.

Presley didn't quite giggle, but it was close. Kane considered his playfulness worth it. He was on a mission to see Presley smile and laugh. It was an honorable mission. A counterbalance to his demands. But also a slippery slope to becoming too invested.

That he could never do, because Kane wasn't built for long term.

But he was built for this. He kept things light for the rest of the meal and enjoyed it when Presley finally got her hands dirty. When they stood to leave, instead of leading the way down the aisle, Kane stepped closer. "I'm glad you had a good time."

Presley had gotten comfortable enough over the last

thirty minutes to raise a sassy eyebrow at him. "What makes you think that?"

Leaning toward her, he snagged a clean napkin from the stack on the table. "Because you actually have sauce on your face."

Her eyes widened, and she glanced around them as if someone would spot her indiscretion and judge.

"Relax," he admonished. "This is a rib place, after all." Then he rubbed the outer edge of her mouth with the napkin, knowing all the while that he really wished it was his mouth on those luscious full lips.

But it was a little too soon to press his luck. Instead he escorted her to the car and took her home like a true gentleman. No one could say he didn't know his place— even though he didn't always stay in it.

After stopping in the drive close to the barn, Kane got out of the SUV. He didn't want to take up the rest of Presley's afternoon, especially since he would be commandeering her evening, but he really wasn't a drop-'em-off-and-drive-away type of guy. Not waiting on him to open her door, she came around the vehicle with a hesitant look on her face. An awkward expression that asked what the heck type of response this situation called for, because she wasn't really sure.

Neither was he. A fact that he found intriguing. Actually, he knew what his response *should* be, but it wasn't what he wanted.

Before either of them could speak, muted shouting erupted from the vicinity of the stables. They shared a startled glance, then took off at a run.

Kane got to the barn first, so he swept the door open

for Presley to sprint through. Half a dozen men stood with a sort of agitated energy at the opening of the stall where he'd first found Presley this morning. A couple of loud thumps emanated from inside. Then Bennett spilled from the darkened doorway with the ranch hand from this morning clinging to him. Not for long, as Bennett unceremoniously dumped the man on the ground.

Bennett stood for a minute with his hands on his hips, watching the man lie there. "There was pretty dang stupid," he finally said.

"What happened?" Presley asked, alerting the group to their presence.

Kane glared when the man on the ground mumbled what he was pretty sure were some choice curse words.

Bennett nodded at the stable hand. "Brilliant here decided to give himself another go at cleaning the mare's hooves. Went even worse than the last time."

"It kicked me," the man ground out.

"Did you deserve it?" Presley asked. "Bennett?"

"Sure did," her stable manager said in a grim tone. "He took a crop to her when she wouldn't stay still."

Everyone tensed. Kane felt the urge to step in, take control and give this idiot a lesson he'd never forget. Just in time, he checked himself. This wasn't his barn. The lesson wasn't his to give—but he would if it wasn't properly learned this time.

The stable hand struggled to his feet. From his movements, Kane guessed the mare had gotten him in the thigh. He was lucky she hadn't caught his knee.

Then the guy had to open his mouth. "Crops are for putting animals in their place."

Yep, he was going to be sore tomorrow…and out of a job.

Presley stepped forward. "Here we use crops sparingly. They are for training and racing—not an instrument of punishment. As a matter of fact, the only place to find one here is in the tack room. Not this stall."

Oh, she was a smart one. Even Kane hadn't caught onto that.

"I refuse to have someone working at Macarthur Haven that I can't trust. Boys, escort him to his truck, please." She stared the injured man down for a moment, matching his glare and almost daring him to say anything more.

Inside, Kane cheered.

"You can come by tomorrow for your gear and final paycheck. Go straight to Bennett and he will supervise your visit."

Apparently that didn't go over well, because the man took a halting step in her direction. He didn't get far. Kane moved forward and blocked his path, arms crossed over his chest to display muscles from years of hard labor, an intent look on his face that dared the man to try any monkey business. Kane didn't even have to speak.

The stable hand immediately lost his steam. Bennett nodded at the group of men, and they ushered the now ex-employee toward the door in a tight formation that brooked no argument.

In minutes, the trouble was under control and Presley thanked Bennett for stepping in before the situation got out of hand.

"I just wish it hadn't occurred at all," he replied with a shake of his head.

"I made my feelings over the treatment of our animals very clear this morning," she said. "Not everyone gets it."

Bennett nodded. He shook Kane's hand, then turned back toward the stall. "I'll check her over and get her settled down."

Presley's heavy sigh told Kane just how much the confrontation had taken out of her. Still... "I'm proud of you for not backing down," he said.

She tossed a surprised look his way, then shrugged. "It's not the first time. Probably not the last. But it's a shame, regardless."

"Does that authoritative stare come naturally, or did you have to cultivate it over the years?"

Her smirk was sassy, sexy. "You may not know this, but if you don't stand up for yourself in a male-dominated environment, they will assume you can't. So I did what was necessary."

"I'm sure your dad was very proud."

Her smile flatlined instantly. "You know, that's the first time you've been wrong about me."

Six

Presley frowned into her rearview mirror as she tried to get her lipstick on without making a mess, for a change. Usually it took her several attempts, when she even bothered to try. Why she was doing this tonight, she wasn't sure. She'd worn nothing but Chapstick for months now. But she did want to look better than usual tonight, even if this was a casual get-together. Thinking back to this afternoon didn't help steady her hand, though.

Her last words to Kane had gone too far, revealed way more than she wished. She'd never talked with anyone about her father's disappointment in her...and he'd never displayed it openly in public. He'd reserved that for his private suggestions to wear a dress instead of pants or to spend more time at the country club than in the barn. While he'd been undeniably proud of her accomplishments, there was no doubt about his disappointment that Marjorie's feminine tendencies hadn't "taken" with Presley. And he had certainly never let her make any final management decisions in the stables, despite her degree and extensive experience.

But she'd kept that secret to herself...until today.

Had Kane seen her as just a little girl whining? He hadn't given any indication, simply studying her for a moment before nodding slightly and turning to go. What did that mean? The man was so hard to read. He kept his reactions close to his chest, leaving her in guessing mode so that when he did let something through—like those occasional glimpses of male interest—she was left to wonder if she'd really understood what had just happened.

The man was blackmailing her! She needed to remember that and stop looking at this like a friendship. Or even worse, a relationship.

One thing was certain: she wasn't getting comfortable with him any time soon. Which would probably suit him fine.

Forcing herself to stop fiddling, Presley got out of her truck and stomped toward the front entrance of the Harrington estate. Of course, the sound wasn't as satisfying when she wasn't wearing her boots. *Dang dress shoes!* And the wait after she rang the bell didn't help her mood. Her stomach churned from nerves as she stood there.

She wasn't quite sure what to expect, but when she heard the word *party*, she wanted to run. Heck, if she was ever lucky enough to get married, she'd probably elope to avoid the ceremony. Because if there was anything worse than a party, it was a party where she was supposed to be the center of attention.

The door swung open, and Presley found herself face-to-face with Kane. His piercing gaze, combined with her thoughts about marriage, sent a flush to her cheeks. Maybe he wouldn't notice it if she stepped in quickly.

"Welcome, Presley."

His deep voice was counterbalanced with EvaMarie's higher one as Presley scooted into the foyer. The light from the sparkling chandelier wasn't as harsh as she'd expected, and EvaMarie's smiling face was a welcome sight. At least she wouldn't be the only woman here.

"Hey, EvaMarie."

From directly behind her, Kane spoke. "What about me?"

Presley hesitated, then glanced over her shoulder. "Oh, hi."

His half grin teased her. "That's a bit more like it, I guess."

"Were you looking for something else?" Was she really flirting with her blackmailer? It kind of felt like it.

Before she could prepare, Kane tucked an arm around her shoulders and pressed his lips against hers. Her squeak reverberated in her own ears, prompting embarrassment to wash over her. He didn't press for more but also didn't back down.

Remembering that this was just business, Presley relaxed. The first sensation to sweep through her was the tingling of her lips. Then the heat where he was touching her thin silky shirt. Both spread across and down like a slow-moving burn. Just as her whole body was engulfed, he pulled back. A mere fraction. Enough for her to feel his breath across her lips.

Then he was gone.

The first thing she saw was EvaMarie's wide-eyed stare. The burn in her cheeks returned. *Great.*

She spent the trip downstairs trying to calm herself. Realizing she was the last to arrive didn't help, but she saw that the only other guests were the Rogers brothers, whom she already knew well. As long as she could keep from embarrassing herself, she'd be okay.

But then again, knowing the other guests as well as she did put her in a bit of a quandary...

"Jake, Steven, this is Presley Macarthur."

"We've known each other since grade school," Jake said, tipping his head at Presley in greeting.

"Most people around here have if they live on the same side of town," EvaMarie confessed to Kane. "Or they at least know of each other."

Presley nodded her own greeting, her attention distracted by the gorgeous antique pool table at the far end of the room. She quickly pulled herself back to the conversation. "How's Princess, Steven?" she asked.

"Good," he said. "That trick you gave me got her back on track. Her speed is up already."

"What trick?" Jake demanded. "Are you holding out on me?"

"You bet I am," Steven said with a grin.

The men mock argued with each other while Mason

helped EvaMarie set up food and drinks on the bar. Kane once again closed in. "Are you gonna share this great trick with me?" he asked in a low voice that gave the question a whole new meaning.

Presley tried to look him in the eyes, she really did. But those lips kept drawing her attention. "Depends."

"On what?"

"On whether you can beat me at pool..."

Did she really say that? For a second, panic pressed hard against Presley's chest, but for once she refused to acknowledge it. If Kane was going to go all in on this Lothario routine, why make it easy for him? He certainly wasn't cutting her any slack. And he seemed to have accepted everything he'd seen of her today— hadn't he?

"That sounds like a challenge," he said, but he didn't look put off by it. Instead, that glitter in his eye seemed to indicate...excitement?

Would nothing go according to plan?

"Shall we play?" Kane announced to the room as a whole.

Presley turned to see the others watching them. Jake raised his empty glass as if in salute. "I think I'll get a drink first. You two go ahead."

As Kane crossed the room to prep the table, Jake shot her a wink—he and Steven were aware of her little talent. She just hoped nerves didn't ruin her performance.

"EvaMarie?" she said, hope lightening her voice.

The other woman gave a soft sigh and wrinkled her nose. "You first," she conceded. "I'm not ashamed to admit I'm horrible."

"And nothing I have done has made her any better," Mason said.

Presley laughed as EvaMarie swatted her fiancé with a towel, then turned toward the pool table with a touch of dread. Kane waited until she got close before holding out a pool stick to her. "Ladies first."

Time to dance.

At least Presley was better at this than regular dancing. Though she was confident in her abilities, she didn't normally perform under the watchful gaze of the most striking man she'd ever met. Drawing in a deep breath, she studied the table, zeroing in on its unfamiliar surface. *Let everything else fade away.* Then she lined up her shot with deliberate care and let loose.

After four successful shots, she glanced up from the far side of the table to see her audience. Jake and Steven chuckled with knowledge of the coup. Mason and EvaMarie exchanged surprised glances. Kane stood almost frozen, brows raised, his gaze trained on the table as if he couldn't figure out what voodoo she was using to accomplish this feat.

Four moves later, the table was clear. With each clink of the balls into the pockets, Presley felt her satisfaction grow. She didn't often get to let her true self out, and it was even rarer for her to enjoy the experience. So this was a treat.

Feeling every ounce of her win, she leaned against the stick and glanced Kane's way. "Guess you won't be finding out that trick today…"

His half grin should have warned her. "Oh, the night isn't over yet, sweetheart."

* * *

Presley smiled as she heard Mason teasing EvaMarie over her pool-playing skills. Presley had enjoyed several games, winning her fair share, but the men had eventually poked some holes in her strategy. As usual, the opposite sex always saw a female pool player as a challenge to be faced and overcome at all odds. At least this group was friendly. Sometimes things could get ugly, which was why she was usually careful about the places she played. And whom she played with.

But now it was time to let someone else be the center of attention—a place Presley never relished.

Crossing back over to the bar, she surveyed the dent already made in the food and started gathering platters.

"You don't have to do that," Kane said as he came up beside her. "I'll take them upstairs for a refill."

"I don't mind helping."

They evenly distributed the serving dishes between them and Kane led the way to the kitchen. The limestone countertop was obviously new, as were the stainless steel appliances. Really nice dark wood floors complemented the red, black and silver color scheme.

"This kitchen is gorgeous."

"Thanks," Kane said as he opened the fridge and started pulling out various containers. "It's not just easier to cook in now, it's a pleasure."

That gave her pause. "You cook?"

"Of course."

She nodded, unsure how deeply she should probe into his actual home life, so she remained silent. Opening the containers and refilling platters at least gave her something to do with her hands.

Luckily Kane volunteered more information so she didn't have to endure the awkward silence much longer.

"EvaMarie and I usually split the duties when I'm here for dinner. If I'm not here, I usually eat out. Doesn't seem to be much point cooking for one, especially after I cooked for grown men for so many years. Mason doesn't have the cooking gene, so I usually fed our hands back home."

Presley thought back to how much she'd seen the stable hands eat on various occasions. Since he'd brought up the subject, maybe she could push a little further. "Yeah, I can see how that would be a big difference. When did you learn to cook?"

Kane refilled the homemade salsa and carefully spread tortilla chips on a platter. "I started when my mom got sick. She and my dad were gone a lot for appointments, and Mason still needed to be fed."

"Very few teenage boys would voluntarily take on that task."

"Well, I'm not gonna say we didn't eat our fair share of frozen pizzas before I figured a few things out. But it had to be done. My mom taught me some things."

And he'd stepped up to the plate.

"Dad wanted me to learn to cook," she admitted.

Kane tilted his head toward her. "You didn't want to learn?"

She barely held back a giggle. "I did try, but nothing good ever came of it."

"That bad?"

"I know it's a disgrace to admit this to an acknowledged cook, but I can't even manage boxed macaroni and cheese."

"Wow," Kane said, slowly shaking his head, but his half grin told her he wasn't judging. "But you obviously have other talents." He nodded toward the basement stairs. "I bet your dad was pretty proud of that."

Presley felt her amusement fade. "Actually, he refused to let me learn how to play pool. He said it wasn't for girls."

Kane raised a brow. The story didn't reflect well on her, but his very silence pressured her to explain.

"He started taking me to horse shows and racing events with him not long after my mother died. But he was very protective. He brought food back to the hotel and didn't go drinking or anything while I was with him. Well, until Marjorie came along—then it was back to staying at home until he decided I was old enough to show horses and compete myself."

She dipped a chip and chewed while she thought back on those times. "One day he left me with one of the newer guys while he went to negotiate the purchase of a horse. The man ordered some takeout food from a local bar. It was the middle of the day, and I got to watch people playing pool while we waited. To my dad's dismay, I was fascinated…"

Again, with the half grin. Why did that look on Kane's face have to be so sexy? "Did the employee get fired?" he asked.

"Close," she remembered. "I think the thing that saved him was he was a young guy who had never dealt with kids before then. And he explained that he'd been afraid to leave me alone while he went for the food."

"Sounds reasonable."

"My dad rarely was reasonable when it came to me. But from then on, billiards, as he called it, was a forbidden subject."

"But you're damn good at it."

She gave a rueful grin. "I learned to play while I was at college—actually took a class. Some of my fellow students started including me in trips to the local pool hall. My dad would have killed me if he saw the place."

"I bet."

"But it sure was fun."

"And you're fun to watch. He missed out."

Presley didn't want to think about that. She'd loved her dad more than anything. Why had he refused to accept so much about her?

"Ready to take this stuff down?" she asked, changing the subject.

Kane laid his hand over hers on the platter. "I'm serious, Presley. This is fun."

"Yeah, for me too." A day hanging out in the barn, lunch at a barbecue dive, then playing pool. Not at all what she'd expected from Kane Harrington. Something told her this was too good to be true.

"One night I'll cook dinner for you."

A sparkle of nerves ignited in her core, warning her this was getting too personal. "Is that part of the agreement?" she asked, suddenly desperate to get them back to business.

"Does it need to be?"

In the kitchen's soft lighting, his dark eyes met hers. Somehow she could tell he didn't care about business—he simply knew what he wanted. But could she trust him?

Could she trust any of this?

Then Mason's voice erupted from downstairs. "Food!"

And Presley was given a reprieve…but not for long. An hour later, Kane insisted on walking her to her car, though she reminded him that the driveway was perfectly safe. Lots of other men would have done the same, and she wouldn't have thought twice about accepting their escort, but being alone with Kane in the dark set those nerves in motion once more.

"I hope you had a good time," he said as they reached her truck.

In the dark, his voice played over her skin, making their conversation feel more intimate than it should. He'd been pleased with her performance tonight. That's all this was.

"You know," she said before she could think too hard about it. "It won't always be this way…" She turned toward him, her back against the driver's side door. "I don't always fit in—okay, I hardly ever fit in."

He seemed to be standing closer than was comfortable, yet she didn't want to push him away. For some reason, she wanted him to know the truth about her.

"I think we'll fit just fine," he said.

"I mean—"

He stepped closer, but somehow they still weren't touching. "I know what you mean. Don't worry about it."

"I've always worried about it," she murmured, distracted by the notion that she wished they *had* touched.

"I know…"

The knowledge in his voice left her worried.

Seven

Kane settled Presley into the front seat of his Escalade, shut the door, then let his grin break through as he skirted the SUV on his way to the driver's side. She'd come to the door with no makeup, her hair in its usual ponytail. For the luncheon of the local chapter of the American Horse Racing Society they were attending, she'd chosen to wear a long skirt with no shape and an equally loose blouse. He didn't even have a description for them except…gray.

Did she even realize how obvious this ploy to remain invisible was? Probably not, since according to EvaMarie she'd been dressing like this for many years. She'd probably forgotten why she started wearing clothes that wouldn't flatter anyone, much less a woman of her natural beauty.

So how would she feel about stop number two today?

He suppressed a grin as he slid behind the steering wheel. He'd worry about that when the objections started—because he knew good and well they would.

Presley chatted pleasantly with the lady at registration when they arrived, then automatically headed in the direction of their table. Those who were already seated smiled and greeted her companionably. He had a feeling she had a set routine at these events that eliminated any unease and minimized any contact with people who would point out her lack of social aptitude.

As she introduced him, he slipped easily into his role of Harrington Farms representative. Even Presley seemed a little dazzled.

The food was above average for a large catered event, and the speaker was interesting. Kane had never actually attended a society event of this caliber. He and Mason had several memberships, but the American Horse Racing Society had certain expectations and heavy entry fees that had kept them out before.

Not a problem now.

The speaker had barely finished when Presley turned to him. "All righty, let's go."

Kane glanced around the room at the small clusters of people forming to signal the usual social hour that followed these types of events. "You don't want to stay?" he asked.

"Um, no." Her raised brows told him how ludicrous the question was.

His little introvert. "Shouldn't we at least speak to Madame President?"

"Right."

He loved the sheepish cast to Presley's expression. It told him so much about the push and pull between her business side and her natural avoidance of anything social, despite her heavily ingrained manners.

Ms. Justine Simone, as Presley introduced her, was every inch a southern maven intent on allowing only limited access to her kingdom until she had more of an idea whom she was letting in.

"Ah, Mr. Harrington. I knew it was only a matter of time before you tried to join our ranks here at the American Horse Racing Society."

"Try?" He gifted her with one of his rare smiles, which he knew had softened up many a detractor. "On the contrary, Ms. Simone, I will *definitely* be joining this lovely organization."

"We shall see about that, Mr. Harrington. We shall see." She smiled, flashing a full set of teeth that rivaled her diamonds in their sparkle. "While I am utterly charmed by handsome men such as yourself, I am a business owner first, and as always, looking out for the good of this organization."

"I do understand."

He could afford to be patient while he grew on her. Eventually, with enough time, he would work magic on those in this room with his natural business acumen and ease in presenting his extensive knowledge. Presley was his key to gaining that time.

Her presence legitimized him in a place where he wouldn't have fit in before, a place where many were accepted based solely on their family name. He, on the other hand, would make a place for himself, regardless of outdated notions of social standing. He'd done it before in his life, and he would do it again as necessary.

"I think you will be suitably impressed," Presley said from his side, drawing the woman's attention her way. "I've been out to the farm, seen the quality of the stock they have already. And I've talked with Kane and his brother, Mason, extensively. Harrington Farms is going to be a premier stable within a few short years— I assure you."

Kane was shocked. Her verbal recommendation wasn't part of the deal. There'd been no requirement for her to sponsor him or endorse him with anything other than her presence. He and Ms. Simone both knew that Presley would never say this if she didn't mean it. Kane found the experience humbling.

"And this young woman would know," Ms. Simone said with a gracious smile in Kane's direction. "I'm not sure her daddy realized what a gem he had in this one. She understands the animal—its needs, its instincts— which is something book learning cannot teach you."

The older woman linked her arm with Presley's. "And she's never been one to be swayed by a pretty face." She threw a discreet wink in Kane's direction. "Not that I would blame her..."

Kane got the distinct feeling Ms. Simone might pinch his cheeks if he stepped any closer.

"And do I hear the infamous Sun might have a hand in building these stables?" Ms. Simone went on.

"He will be a part of the bloodline, yes," Presley

admitted, her sudden stillness making him aware of a growing tension in her body.

She could have said no. She could have said there was a misunderstanding. She could have told him Kane was on his own. Instead she was championing his case in a way he hadn't asked for, which was sweeter and sexier than if she'd offered him something else—something he shouldn't be thinking about in this setting.

"So he isn't being sold?" Ms. Simone asked sweetly, though Kane could see her sly quest for knowledge.

He easily set her straight. "A simple miscommunication. Sun has been with Presley since he was weaned. That would be like selling part of the family."

He returned Presley's wide-eyed gaze with steady calm. What happened before was between the two of them. He wasn't even sure he could change that if he needed to, since his growing instinct was to protect her. Standing here, sharing this connection with her, he acknowledged the truth.

This was deeper than he'd planned.

"What are we doing here?"

Kane frowned. He'd expected objections once they got inside the town's most exclusive clothing store, but he hadn't expected the battle to start in the parking lot. And they'd been having such a pleasant afternoon...

"I need to pick up my tux for the gala at the museum this weekend."

Presley crossed her arms firmly over her stomach. Her set expression wasn't encouraging. "I'll wait here."

"Why?"

She frowned. "Why not?"

Kane relaxed back into his seat, giving Presley his full attention. Her fists clenched, suggesting she wasn't happy about that, either. "Don't you want to see what I'm wearing? Make sure we don't clash or anything?"

"Is that really a thing outside of prom?"

"Look, I don't have all day," he said, cutting to the chase. "Why don't you just tell me what's wrong so we can move on."

"So we can move on? Seriously?"

"Yes."

Her expression conveyed shock over his stubbornness, but Kane wasn't budging. This behavior had gone on too long. If her daddy couldn't break her of it, he sure as heck would.

"I'm waiting, Presley."

She scrunched her eyebrows together. "Just go get your tux."

"Not happening." He kept his gaze steady and serious.

This trick worked pretty well on Presley. "I don't like this store."

"This store? Or this *type* of store?" He needed to be sure about what he was dealing with here.

"Well, I'm not thrilled about any formal dress store," she said tartly, "but this one is a particular nuisance to me."

Kane glanced at the front of the stately building modeled after the style of the elegant manor houses dotting this end of town. "Someone recommended this store to me as one of the oldest in town, with the best reputation."

Looking back at Presley, he could see a slight wobble in the stubborn tilt of her chin. "Mrs. Rose has been very helpful and attentive every time I've been in here."

"I don't care."

"I do. Spit it out."

Presley rolled her eyes at his masculine ultimatum, but he didn't miss the glint of moisture before she blinked.

"Marjorie insisted on buying all the clothes for her and Dad's wedding here. We came. I sat. Marjorie shopped with her girlfriends. It was a horrid experience, repeated often."

He glanced back at the building. "You refuse to go inside because you were forced to shop here as a kid? Seems extreme to me."

"Well…"

He waited. He was good at that.

"The last time she brought me here was for a fitting for my bridesmaid's dress. I was a token junior bridesmaid so they could say I had actually been included in the wedding." Presley rubbed her palms down her skirt, stretching the material. "It was an awful froufrou dress with multiple layers of ruffles for a skirt. I felt like one of those Barbie cakes in that stupid thing. When I refused to wear it, Marjorie and I got into a yelling match in the store."

"That must have been embarrassing."

"Not at the time, but I've never been back. Marjorie got tired of me fussing, so she shook me by the shoul-

ders. I pulled away and fell right into a rack of jew-
elry. Knocked the whole thing over and tore my dress
when I fell."

"Let me guess? You didn't have to wear it?"

She worried her lower lip between her teeth, but a
smile threatened to break free. "I'm ashamed to say I
did not. The new dress wasn't as comfortable as jeans,
but Mrs. Rose picked out something much simpler."

"But you've still never been back?"

"Would you go back? After behaving that way?"

"You were a child. You're a grown woman now.
Right?"

She gave him a wary look. And she was right to be
suspicious. But he wasn't backing down.

"So let's go."

Kane gave her the space to hang back as they went
through the front door with its delicate chime and down
a ramp into the heart of southern-formal world. Mrs.
Rose herself stood talking to a younger woman behind
the counter. Her little wrinkled face lit up when she saw
him. "Mr. Harrington! I've been impatiently waiting for
you and Ms. Macarthur to arrive."

She rounded the counter with a much sprier step
than one would anticipate from a seventysomething. "I
have the most wonderful selection for her to try on—"

The sharp, choked note from behind him caught the
older woman's attention. "Hello, Ms. Macarthur," the
proprietress said with a beaming smile. "It's lovely to
see you in my store again."

Kane glanced back over his shoulder and almost

choked himself at Presley's glare. He was busted. But this would be good for her. She'd see.

Mrs. Rose didn't seem to notice the silent communication. "I'm so excited," she prattled on. "I see your mother in here often, but never you."

Kane saw Presley's lips tighten when Marjorie was mentioned and silently applauded her for not correcting the older woman's description.

"And your tuxedo is ready for your fitting, Mr. Harrington."

Kane nodded as they followed Mrs. Rose farther into the store. He would try on the clothes later. Leaving Presley by herself right now wasn't a good idea.

They came to a small sitting area. Mrs. Rose gestured for them to be seated on a plush semicircular bench. "I'll just go get everything ready," she said before scurrying away.

Presley glanced at the bench then turned away with a shudder. Kane figured he'd be better off meeting her resistance on his feet. The blows weren't long in coming.

"I thought we were getting your tux," she said, her sharp tone giving him a good gauge of her temper levels.

"And I asked if you wanted us to match."

"No, no, I don't. I want to be the least—" she stared at him in frustration, obviously searching for the words she wanted "—matchy couple there."

If her temper made her any cuter, he was going to do something that might make her head explode. "So are you gonna be rude to a sweet little lady and not try on her clothes?" he asked, attempting to stay calm and not give in to his amusement.

"Yes." Presley glanced around at the overflow of dresses and mirrors. "No."

Kane simply nodded. "It is a conundrum."

The sound that came from her throat was suspiciously like a growl, but before he could respond, Mrs. Rose returned and gestured them toward a separate fitting area along the back wall. More privacy, as Kane had requested.

"This way," she said smartly. "We're all ready."

As Kane studied the tight, straight line of Presley's back, he couldn't help thinking some of them were more ready than others.

Eight

Presley stared at the rows of dresses hanging on the rack in front of her as if they were snakes. Actually, that wasn't true. Snakes she knew how to handle. Ambushes at local formal boutiques…not so much.

She should have known better than to start thinking Kane was a guy who might just accept her for the person she was. Instead they had their first formal public appearance tomorrow night, and he'd done the unthinkable. She hadn't looked at even one dress, and already anger and embarrassment were building.

She had a feeling making a scene wouldn't work as well with Kane as it had with her stepmother.

Honestly, she'd let her inner angry child show way too much today. She didn't like flashing her issues around like a sign that her world had been screwed up long before her father died. The few times they'd discussed her family, Kane had been understanding. At the moment, though, she got the feeling he was laughing at her, leaving Presley to feel like a child throwing a tantrum.

Maybe that's what she was…

She could be an *adult* about this. She'd try on a few dresses, decline them, then they'd be on their way. She nodded to herself, ignoring the dozen or so candidates waiting on the rack. Good strategy.

"Let's get started, shall we?" Mrs. Rose said, grabbing a surprisingly large armful for such a small woman and heading into a dressing room that had the curtain thrown back away from the entrance.

Presley sheepishly followed, watching as Mrs. Rose arranged her choices on another, smaller rack. Not a ruffle in sight, much to Presley's relief. Also none of the pale colors she gravitated toward. A wide array of jewel tones hung before her, begging for attention.

The very thing Presley did not want.

She stared long after Mrs. Rose left, drawing the curtain closed behind her. Where should she start? Should she start at all? What in the world was she doing here?

Just as her insides started to shake, she heard Kane from right outside the curtain.

"Let me see them, Presley."

"No." Her voice had a way-too-embarrassing squeak in it.

Without another word, Kane pulled the curtain back, just enough to stick his head through.

"What are you doing?" she hissed.

"You *will* let me see you in the dresses," he insisted. Though his voice was only loud enough for her to hear, it still carried the weight of authority. "If you don't, I'll just pull the curtain back at random moments and the whole store can listen to you squeal."

In desperation, she glanced at the edge of the curtain in search of a way to keep it closed, but there was none.

Kane chuckled. "No lock to keep me out, sweetheart."

He was enjoying this—and unfortunately for her, she knew he would follow through on his threat. No matter how much embarrassment that would cause her.

"Or I could simply come in and help."

Presley's mouth went dry. Visions of him wrangling a dress over her head made her cringe. That wasn't the way she wanted him to see her naked the first time.

Not that she wanted him to see her naked at all. Absolutely not.

Shoot, who was she kidding?

"I'm not gonna like this," she said through gritted teeth.

"Look at me," Kane said, his voice going dark and serious.

She found herself compelled to obey.

"Trust me. I think you'll be pleasantly surprised."

By him invading her dressing room? That might be the only fun thing to come out of this.

"I'll be out in a minute," she said, ignoring the flames licking her cheeks.

Hearing him chuckle on the other side of the curtain didn't make her feel any better.

Blindly she reached out and grabbed the first dress

she touched. Taking off her clothes left her feeling vulnerable, but oddly stimulated. Knowing Kane was on the other side of the curtain with full knowledge of what she was doing had her brain sending out tingling signals of awareness.

Stop. It.

This situation was hard enough without adding unwanted arousal to the mix. One look in the mirror made her sigh. She hated trying on clothes. Hated looking at herself in the mirror. Clothing was functional for her. The rest was a mystery.

"Presley, now."

At least he didn't sound like he was standing right outside. When she pulled the curtain back, she saw him leaning casually against a pillar behind one of the padded benches nearby. She forced herself not to wrap her arms around her middle and tried to avoid any other self-conscious gestures.

"What do you think?" he asked, his tone and expression neutral.

She'd barely looked in the mirror, but the sight was burned into her retinas. "Not a big fan," she said with a grimace.

"Why?"

Her defenses were up, but his stance remained neutral. "I like green, but this shade reminds me of Jolly Ranchers. And I have no idea what to do with this." She waved the ends of a sash in the air.

Kane's lips twitched. "I agree. Green is a good color for you, but not this one. Next."

Presley blinked, not moving. Most people—the few

she'd ever let go shopping with her—spent their time arguing as to why a particular piece was right for her, despite her protests. This was new.

He didn't change his mind. He just stared with raised brows until she turned away. Presley couldn't get her mind to process what had just happened, so she pulled out another dress and robotically started the complicated process of getting it on.

Three was usually her limit for items she was willing to try on before grabbing the loosest thing in the vicinity and rushing to the checkout counter. But Kane's opinions on everything she came out in fascinated her. She actually started looking through the options and picking things that might work instead of just grabbing the next in line.

And then she found it.

First, the blue definitely complimented the green color of her eyes—even she could see that. Second, it slid on easily, without any complicated pieces and parts. And third, she could actually see her shape in it without feeling like she was in a full-body stranglehold.

The silky material followed her curves like water running over her skin. There were actually multiple layers, which gave the silhouette a little movement without twisting, another major annoyance of hers.

It was beautiful.

Presley held her breath as she came out of the dressing room this time. Afraid she was wrong, afraid he would hate it…simply afraid.

Kane held still for long moments, studying her with that inscrutable look he got sometimes. Then he took her hand and led her to a raised platform before a three-way mirror toward the back of the little alcove. The added height almost allowed her to look him straight in the eyes. The mirror let her watch as he stepped up onto the platform behind her.

She felt him fumbling with the hair tie holding her ponytail. As he released it, her heart started to pound. Still in fear, but also…anticipation. The thick weight of her hair spread across her shoulders. Seeing Kane's long fingers in the mass sparked a feeling of intimacy, almost as if he were undressing her.

Then those same fingers skimmed downward, tracing the hourglass shape revealed by the material, leaving a trail of goose bumps in their wake.

"Do you feel comfortable?" he finally asked, a deep note in his voice she couldn't recognize but that she wanted to hear more of.

Unable to put words to what she was feeling, she simply nodded.

"Restricted?"

"No," she whispered, as if the word was a betrayal of her long-held clothing beliefs.

He stepped back down off the platform, then returned with a shoe box. Presley could barely hear for the blood rushing in her ears. *Please, don't ruin this.*

She wasn't quite sure if the plea was for her or for him. Kneeling before her, Kane lifted an especially sparkly sandal from the box, then held out a hand for her foot. She had to lift her skirt up, and her psyche flooded with the sense of exposing secrets to the dark man before her. Her hands clenched into the material, but she didn't resist as he lifted her foot and slid the shoe onto it. The warmth of his palm against her ankle increased that sudden sense of intimacy.

After securing both shoes, he returned to stand behind her. "Do the shoes hurt?"

The slight kitten heel felt a little odd. She was used to either flats or boots. But the heels weren't high enough that she was afraid she would fall. The straps were soft on the inside, not rubbing like most of the dress shoes she endured for these events. "No. They're pretty."

The view in the mirror entranced her for a moment. The bright brilliant blue of her dress and her blond hair stood out in contrast to Kane's dark good looks and black dress shirt and jeans. But it was the look in his eyes that caught and held her attention. Definitely lust. She'd never seen it directed at her, but she recognized it nonetheless. But there was also something else. Something just as brilliant as the color of her dress.

Understanding, maybe?

His fingers returned to her hair, testing the texture in long, soft strokes. "I've always felt that dressing up isn't about changing—it's about creating an enhanced version of who you really are."

"So you're speaking from experience?" she asked quietly, her tone almost hushed in the intimate space between them.

His half grin made a reappearance, but it didn't reach his dark eyes. "I didn't grow up with money, Presley. My version of formal clothes was a new pair of jeans once a year." His gaze shifted to his reflection in the mirror. "This new reality took me a while to wrap my head around. But I am who I've made myself—no one else."

His hands rested lightly on her shoulders. "You can present anything you want to the world, Presley," he continued. "Dressing down was your quiet form of rebellion. But your father isn't here anymore. Now is the time to let it go."

The next evening, in her bedroom, Presley stared at her face in the mirror, more than a little shocked.

Once she'd chosen a few dresses, Mrs. Rose had introduced her to a young woman at the store tasked with showing her how to put on makeup, and all her childish protests had risen once more.

"I really don't like the feel of makeup on my skin," she'd objected. Which was the truth. And only one of the reasons she'd never learned to put any on. The horses and stable hands didn't care, so why should she?

"Oh, you don't need it all over," the young woman had assured her. "You have gorgeous skin. I can just show you a few ways to give yourself a more polished look for formal occasions."

Skepticism rode her hard, but Presley had decided there wasn't any harm in letting the woman have her way. She could just wash it off when she got home—before Marjorie could see.

But she hadn't. Not only that, she'd been able to replicate the techniques today with minimal effort.

Following the step-by-step instructions, Presley had added the exact colors to the exact places they needed to go, then rubbed a bigger brush over her lids, resulting in some pretty shading that made her green eyes stand out even more. She'd finished with a barely there dusting of blush that gave her face some color and sheer, dark pink gloss that emphasized the curves of her lips.

Seeing herself in the mirror had her straightening her back, smiling a little. Polished? Yeah, that was the right word.

Now she crossed to the bed and got dressed with enough excitement and nerves that her fingers shook slightly. She couldn't help imagining what people would say tonight. She'd always hated being the center of attention, but tonight would be different.

Kane was right. Not caring about her appearance was her own form of rebellion against her father, Marjorie, and their insistence that she should be more feminine. But it was time to move on to another phase of her life.

She held up a pretty pair of panties and studied the matching bra on the bed. Luckily, Mrs. Rose had banished Kane to try on his tux before breaking out the undergarments yesterday, but at that point Presley had been in a pliable enough mood to go with the flow. In line with what she'd already seen Presley pick out, Mrs. Rose hadn't presented a full seductress line of lingerie, just some simple, pretty support pieces with an ultrasoft texture Presley fell in love with immediately. She'd ordered a full range to be delivered with the dresses she'd chosen.

Which made her both proud and slightly ashamed—because she couldn't help wondering if Kane would see them on her…or not.

The desire she'd seen on his face had been very real, but that didn't mean he would ever act on it.

She couldn't help noticing that getting dressed tonight was just as quick as throwing on jeans and tucking in a T-shirt, all thanks to Kane's acceptance of her clothing quirks and Mrs. Rose's efforts to find things that worked for her. No matter how this all started, she had a feeling she would end up owing Kane far more than the money her stepmother had taken for Sun.

Seeing the lights from Kane's SUV flash across the front of the house at dusk, she hurried out the front door and down the stone steps. The clack of her jeweled kitten heels was unfamiliar, but it added to a slight Cinderella feeling. For the first time she could remember, Presley felt like a woman from head to toe. The swish of her hair, thick and loose around her shoulders, made her wonder if Kane would touch it again.

In the dim light outside, she watched as Kane cataloged her new look as she approached him. She'd picked out a cocktail dress for tonight's event. The jewel-green dress had a flowy skirt that hit right at her knees and a blousy top with slits in the sheer arms. An elastic waist added to the comfort, but a jeweled attachment looked like a belt around the front without the tight confinement of one.

It was the most comfortable dress she'd ever put on, but it didn't look as though comfort was the goal of wearing it.

Kane let out a low wolf whistle. "You chose well," he added.

She should have been offended, but she'd never been

whistled at before, and his response made her warm all over. Which was something she should definitely ignore. "Only with your help. You knew good and well I'd never pick this or any of the other dresses out for myself," she said, not quite able to attain her desired tartness in the face of his appreciation.

"Or any dress in that store," he replied, softening his know-it-all attitude by kissing the back of her hand after helping her into the passenger seat.

But he didn't go over the top with the attention. As soon as he settled behind the wheel, conversation returned to normal. If he'd made a big deal out of her transformation, she would have felt uncomfortable—but then, the insufferable man probably knew that as well.

Instead he started talking about a mare at Harrington Farms that was about ready to foal. Then they discussed some training techniques she'd been researching. But on the drive, Kane threw more than a couple of admiring glances her way.

Presley returned more than a few of her own. Kane didn't look so bad himself. The tux he'd purchased fit him to perfection, squaring off across his broad shoulders then skimming the muscles of his back, pulling a little as he gripped the wheel. Her awareness of him grew until she could sense his every movement without even looking in his direction. The occasional whiff of a barely there cologne and the low timbre of his voice in the darkened car only set her further along the edge of arousal.

At least the sensations distracted her from her nerves. Thoughts of whether people would notice her and make comments left her stomach a little hollow. She didn't want to be in the spotlight, but she was also tired of fading into the background. Their time at Mrs. Rose's formal shop had taught her that much. But that didn't mean she wanted people making a big deal of her transformation—especially Marjorie, who had left for the party a full hour before her so she could enjoy cocktails with some friends.

Luckily the first faces they saw as they walked into the marble rotunda of the museum were Mason and EvaMarie.

"Hello," EvaMarie greeted them, her smile widening as she took in Presley's new look. "Wow. You look great."

"Thank you," Presley said, her cheeks stinging until the conversation moved on. Surreptitiously she took a deep breath, trying to calm herself. It was just a dress, for goodness' sake.

No big deal.

Things settled into a more normal rhythm as EvaMarie asked about the association luncheon the day before, though Presley noticed that Mason kept shifting from one foot to the other. Was he nervous about something, too?

A few new arrivals joined them, and Presley weathered another round of questions about her dress more easily this time. She managed okay but quickly lost interest when the other women embraced fashion as a full-on topic. Presley was proud of her clothes, but she wasn't at all interested in discussing them. Her glance around told her that the two men had abdicated the discussion themselves, stepping to the side to hold a private conversation.

Presley was ashamed of her curiosity, but a lifetime of eavesdropping to learn things people wouldn't tell her came in handy sometimes.

"Why won't you talk about this with me?" Mason demanded of his brother.

Kane's tone didn't match Mason's intensity. "What's to tell?"

"Well, your ex-fiancée got married. No one should have to find that out via email, Kane."

Shock held Presley very still, very quiet. On an intellectual level, she recognized that this was a piece of gossip that hadn't been passed around in their social circles. After all, Marjorie would surely have mentioned if Kane had been engaged before now.

But on a personal level, her curiosity grew. What kind of woman wouldn't want Kane? *Why* had she not wanted Kane?

"There's no need to make such a big deal out of things," Kane insisted. "So she got married. So what?"

Apparently he wasn't interested in answering his brother's questions, just deflecting them. Which meant she had a snowball's chance in hell of finding out what she shouldn't want to know in the first place.

"This is a really big deal," Mason continued, not seeming fazed by his brother's lack of response. "He's our business manager, and has been for over fifteen years. Of course he's worried about you. He called to make sure you would handle finding out okay."

"Notice he didn't call me."

"Because he didn't want his head chewed off." Even in his low tone, Presley could tell Mason was both irritated and laying the sarcasm on thick.

Kane didn't respond. Presley ached to turn in their direction, away from the distracting nuisance of the women talking fashion right in front of her, but instinctively she knew the brothers' conversation would end the minute that happened. As sad as it made her, she wanted to know more.

"Seriously," Mason finally continued, "he's worried. After the accident and everything that happened, I'm worried."

"I don't understand why." Kane's words were short, clipped.

Mason wasn't put off. "Because I know you aren't made of stone. After she was hurt, you just shut down. But now—look, are you okay?"

Nothing. Presley couldn't stand the pressure, the anticipation. Finally, she turned to look at the men, but Kane was walking away.

Nine

Is she trying to kill me?

Kane couldn't miss the woman in green as he stepped into the ballroom. Instead of looking like a drab bird, she stood out from the crowd. Not just because of the color of her dress, but because of the sheer glow about her. The extra attention might have made her nervous at first, but that was rapidly changing.

He couldn't even take the credit. Once they'd gotten over her initial reluctance, she'd taken matters into her own hands. The results were simple and stunning, as he'd suspected they would be.

One thing was for sure: she was definitely seducing him, without even trying.

And it was so much more pleasant than thinking about Emily, the specter Mason had brought to the party. She had no place here. Not anymore. Kane only needed Presley—closer, right now.

Without thought, he crossed directly to her, clasped her hand and led her to the dance floor. His own dance style was simple, so he was able to focus on her nearness, the feel of her. He could hear the fabric of her dress swish against his pant legs. He could feel the movement of her body beneath his palm. Every sense tuned in; he was desperate to soak in her essence.

If he had his way, he would experience all that was Presley Macarthur before the night was done.

As if she felt it, too, she glanced up to meet his gaze. Her eyes were wide, vulnerable, and Kane could see an answering need reflecting back at him. "How much longer until we can leave?" he mumbled.

A wine-colored blush spread across her cheeks, telling him he was right, even as she dropped her gaze and worried her lower lip with the edge of her teeth. Without thinking, he let his feet stop, drew her in close and conveyed his desire with a kiss. It felt so good to slide his hands up the back of her neck and into the thickness of her hair. The return pressure and slight parting of her lips told him she felt the same.

Surely it was time to go now...

Unfortunately he didn't see the obstacle before there was enough time to avoid it.

"Presley, oh, my goodness!"

Marjorie stepped right into their path, blocking Kane's progress toward the door. "Look at you. I almost didn't recognize you properly dressed up for a change. So beautiful."

Kane felt Presley's automatic withdrawal, and not just because of the closed expression on her face and the step backward she took.

"And you, Kane," Marjorie continued in an overly loud voice that made Kane want to cringe on Presley's behalf, "aren't you the most handsome man here? Isn't it nice she's finally made an effort to be worthy of being seen with you?"

What was this woman's problem? And how could she not see the effect she was having on Presley? No wonder Presley had adopted whatever strategy she could to keep Marjorie at arm's length.

"Presley doesn't need to make an effort—" he started.

"Nonsense. I've been telling her she needs to make an effort her entire life. Not that she would listen," Marjorie finished.

Then a new voice entered the conversation. "Oh, we all tried." Joan Everly's singsong cadence ramped up Kane's irritation. "But sometimes growing up takes a while."

Kane wondered if he imagined Presley's step closer to his side.

Marjorie, however, smiled at the newcomer. "Well, I know who I have to thank for that," she said, pointing in Kane's direction. "Why, I haven't seen her covered in horse manure in days. I can't believe someone has finally taught her how to be womanly."

The target of Marjorie's comment remained silent. But not Joan.

"Let's hope he hasn't taught her too many things," she mumbled, loud enough for Kane to still hear her.

Marjorie's nonexistent brows shot up.

"Of course, I never had to be taught," Joan continued, turning her gaze directly toward Kane. "To be feminine, that is. It's always come naturally to me."

Kane was very careful not to drop his gaze, because if he wasn't mistaken, little Joan was arching her back to put her cleavage more on display.

"But Presley was always a horsey girl, you know." She glanced at the object of her ridicule with a small smile. "I doubt it will be long before she's back in jeans."

Just then, the hand tucked into his slipped away.

"Oh, goodness, I hope not," Marjorie said. "Leave a woman some hope."

Kane reached out and found Presley's hand once more. He kept his grip firm. She wasn't getting away, and he wanted her to know it.

"Actually, I hope she's back in jeans tomorrow," he interjected. "It would be silly to work in a dress in a barn. And since Presley is the reason Macarthur Haven is still kicking, I'd think you might change your mind about that, too, *Marjorie*."

His pointed look actually had the older woman's cheeks filling with ruddy color. *Let her remember exactly what her stepdaughter is doing for her.*

Finally, he glanced Presley's way, keeping quiet until she raised her gaze to meet his. It wasn't for long, just a few seconds before it dropped again, but maybe it was enough for her to see the truth. A truth he wasn't hiding any longer.

He wanted her.

"Presley and I have gotten to know each other very well," he said, leaving the women to decide what he meant. "She's an excellent business manager, animal lover and daughter. I didn't teach her anything. I simply gave her permission to be her best self."

He turned a piercing gaze on Joan. "There's more to a woman than a dress," he said, not bothering to hide his annoyance. "If not, what's the point in hanging around?"

There was no stopping it. His own wicked way of looking at things wouldn't be held back. So he said the very thing he knew would get into Joan's craw. "Besides, Presley is sexy no matter what she's wearing... or not wearing, for that matter."

He quickly sidestepped the two women as if they were an unwanted encumbrance and led Presley on a single-minded trek to the front doors. She didn't protest. Didn't say anything, in fact. By now, she should have been talking smack, but she wasn't.

That's what worried him.

Presley wasn't sure how long she'd been riding in the SUV, shaking on the inside, concentrating on not letting the tremors show. As she became more aware of her surroundings, she also realized that her feelings weren't as cut-and-dried as they should be.

She'd been subjected to ridicule from Joan since the moment Joan realized just how powerful it made her feel. Of course, normally her taunts were more veiled and more private. Presley had overlooked the comments about her clothing choices and lack of ability to compete on any kind of sexual level for what seemed like forever. Their potency had been weakened by years of repetition.

But not tonight. For some reason, knowing Kane wasn't just the witness but the recipient of Joan's comments changed everything. Joan's first words had made her heart pound, but everything else was now lost in a red sea of embarrassment. As if Marjorie and Joan had stripped her naked so they could point out all of her flaws—to Kane.

He wasn't the type to walk away. Oh, no. Instead he'd defended her—she remembered every word of that part of the exchange in detail. But she wished she couldn't.

Presley and I have gotten to know each other very well...

"Why would you tell them that?" she choked.

She could feel Kane glance her way in the dark, but she didn't turn to look at him.

"Which part?" he asked.

You don't remember, because it doesn't affect you. "They're going to think we're sleeping together," she mumbled, almost afraid to say the words aloud. But a force deep inside—maybe anger, maybe need— wouldn't let her stay quiet any longer.

Kane wasn't helping. "So?"

"The season's just started." Why was she pursuing this line of questions? It could only lead to an embarrassing rejection. Right? "Do you really want to keep this pretense up for months on end?"

"Will it be a pretense?" he asked.

For a moment, her breath caught in her throat. "What?"

Instead of answering, Kane turned the wheel, then pressed on the brakes. Presley's stomach lurched as the SUV jerked and went still. Kane twisted in his seat to face her.

"I haven't made any secret of the fact that I'm attracted to you, Presley."

She shook her head as if to deny what she already knew. "But I thought that was…" Her throat closed.

In the lights from the dash, Kane looked even darker, more dangerous and determined. "I have absolutely no need to pretend," he said. "This is me, Presley. I'll always be honest with you."

She thought back to all he'd told her since they'd first met. *And by the way, if there should be any side effects to our spending time together—mutual consent…* The doubt returned, clouding her thinking.

"Did you say all that just to get in my pants?"

His chuff of laughter made her ears burn. "No. I said it because it's the truth. But while we're talking, is it working?"

"Is what?"

"My attempt to get in your pants."

"Of course it is."

Did she really just say that? She should have been embarrassed; she should backtrack. Instead the internal pressure from earlier faded away, leaving only an aching need for him to be telling the truth.

"Good," he said simply, then reached across the console for her.

Presley didn't resist, couldn't resist. Her lips met his halfway, eager for another taste of Kane's dark essence.

His kiss was soft yet strong. Eager and hungry. Anticipation swelled to match the pounding of her blood. Kane's hand slid up into her hair, burying deep in the loose thickness, holding her still for his thorough exploration.

It wasn't the overzealous fumbling of a boy, but the firm lead of a man who knew what he wanted. His tongue teased along the seam of her lips, and she allowed him inside. He conquered every new inch of territory with a sensual purpose that allowed her to concentrate on the way he made her feel.

Suddenly Kane pulled back, breathing hard as he rested his forehead against hers. His fingers flexed against the back of her skull, eliciting a moan from deep in her throat. His obvious struggle for control sent a thrill rushing through her. No one had responded to a simple kiss with her like that—certainly not someone as strong and single-minded as Kane.

For the first time, she heard Kane erupt into full-bodied, rolling laughter. Everything in her froze, almost waiting for the *gotcha* like an awkward high school girl lured under the bleachers, only to find herself the object of ridicule. Instead, Kane wiped a hand over his eyes, then gestured toward the windshield.

"Apparently my subconscious knows what I want, too."

Huh? Her gaze followed the light, and she blinked

for a moment, then suppressed a smile. Illuminated in the glow of the headlights was the columned porch of Kane's house in town.

The walk into Kane's house wasn't nearly as uncomfortable as it was once she got inside. Presley wished she could go back to the mindless passion of moments ago, instead of feeling the self-conscious awareness that they were moving into territory that had never worked out for her the way it was depicted in romantic movies.

Kane secured the front door, then asked quietly as he removed her wrap, "Would you like a drink?"

"Yes. No."

Ugh.

Kane grinned at her. "Not sure, huh?"

"Well, yes, I feel the need for one, but not for a good reason. No, I don't want one, because then I might not be as in control as I need to be and…" She breathed in deep. "I'm rambling."

The way he studied her made her feel even more uncomfortable. Why did she have to be so socially awkward? Give her a room full of guys wanting to hear step-by-step instructions on how to bit train a horse, and she could give them exactly what they wanted. Give her one man in a room with passion on his mind, and she completely flaked out and failed to deliver.

This was her experience of womanhood…

Kane offered his trademark half grin and took her hand, leading her up the stairs that rose along the left side of the foyer. "Don't worry," he said. "I don't think you'll need alcohol to have a good time."

"I hope you feel the same later," she mumbled.

He didn't even hesitate but continued upward.

Please, please don't let him be disappointed.

Her heart pounded, and she felt as far from aroused as possible by the time they reached Kane's bedroom. She distracted herself by examining the surroundings: antique wooden floors, a tapestry of a hunting scene over the fireplace, the heavy mahogany bed frame and furniture against the creamy walls.

A small lamp from the hallway let her see inside, but Kane didn't move to turn on any more lights. *Thank goodness.* Her stomach churned. Kane's presence surrounded her from behind. She could feel him finger individual strands of her hair and wanted so badly to close her eyes, to slip under his spell.

But she was afraid. This was one area where confidence in her job would not help her.

But then those big hands began to knead her shoulders, her neck, her scalp, and liquid sparkles melted into her blood. By the time he released the single clasp on the back of her dress, she was beyond protest.

The dress could only come off over her head, but that didn't seem to worry Kane. She felt the brush of him against her back, then warm palms pressed against her naked thighs. He traced up and over the curve of her hips, cupping them so his fingers cradled her hip bones. His fingers lay just inches from the part of her body that told her in no uncertain terms this was what she wanted.

Her body jerked involuntarily. Kane's hold tightened. Then, to her surprise, he guided her back against him.

His thigh pressed firmly against that most intimate part of her, eliciting a rush of need. Presley didn't know whether to be grateful or regretful of the clothes still separating them. The urgency to feel Kane's skin, all over, grew with each touch.

But he made it clear he was running this show.

He guided her in a rocking motion until her breath was shallow and staggered. Then those wicked palms moved farther upward, taking her dress with them, until the only thing covering her most intimate parts was a thin, silky pair of panties.

The dress continued inching up her body, until the sheer momentum lifted her arms. Then it was over her head and her hair fell back around her shoulders. Kane didn't leave her time to be self-conscious.

One moment he was glued to her, then he was gone. Before she had time to think, he swept her up in his arms and strode to the bed. This was definitely new... He came down with her until Presley felt surrounded by the heat and musk of him. He buried his face against her neck.

Presley found herself staring at the darkened ceiling as the sensation of Kane's open mouth on her skin left a trail of fire. A sudden awareness of his clothes brushing over her bare skin flooded through her. Soft with just a touch of starch, the fabric of his shirt made every one of her nerve endings take notice. The knowledge that she lay beneath him in just bra and panties while he was fully clothed left her vulnerable, yet...not.

Closing her eyes, she concentrated on the sensations.

She grabbed his upper arms, her fingers digging into the muscle as she pulled him closer.

"Yes, Presley," he groaned against her skin.

Suddenly she wanted to give him her all, not just lie there waiting on him.

She reached farther, burying her fists into the back of his shirt. Though she pulled against him, he didn't fall, but his body began to rock. She recognized the motion from earlier, but the full-on version was a whole different experience. A preview of exactly where they were headed. Kane's sucking kisses moved down her collarbone to her cleavage, causing her nipples to tighten in almost painful need.

Her grasping hands moved to his collar, then around to the buttons. But she wasn't dexterous enough for this particular exercise at the moment. No problem. Kane reared up to balance on his knees, then jerked his shirt open from collar to hem.

His urgency echoed her own, and a small part of her sighed in relief, finally letting go of the self-conscious worry that he was somehow only humoring her.

He didn't try for her bra clasp, but instead pulled the cups down to expose her shaking breasts. Her cries filled the dim room as he teased first one nipple then the other in a synchronized dance that brought them to taut red points. Presley snaked her hands between them until her fingers found his belt buckle.

Then Kane stilled. Presley's breath caught. Was he upset? Frustrated? She could feel the press of his hardness against the backs of her knuckles.

"Unzip me," he demanded.

Her sudden tension melted, and her fingers fumbled before finally achieving her goal. Kane's hand brushed hers away to complete the task of freeing himself. Watching Kane kneel between the vee of her legs to yank down his pants was gratifying in the extreme.

Eager and ready, Kane reached for Presley's panties. She expected him to yank them down or something. Instead his fingers slid around the edge, and Presley's world zeroed in on the feel of him brushing against her wetness. He bent close and breathed against her through the fabric. Presley's heart pounded hard; her hips lifted as her need spiked.

Then the rip came, and Presley's new panties were nothing but shredded fabric. Kane covered himself quickly. Then her. Nothing could have prepared her for the feel of his hardness pressing against her, into her. Presley reached for his hips without thought, only aching need. One hard pull of her hands, and he drove into her.

Her back arched. Her head strained back as everything within her tightened around him. Kane's deep, guttural groans filled her senses. Then his weight came down on her as he started to pump.

Time and space gave way to sensation. The heat of his body. The smell of musk and cologne. The rough texture of his skin against her inner thighs. The delicious pressure of his body inside hers.

Kane shifted up on his arms, and the change made Presley's world explode. She had a vague sense of the frantic working of his hips and a sudden pressure as he cried out. It was all wrapped up in the intense wonder of the moment as Kane collapsed into Presley's arms.

For a brief moment in time, everything was perfect in her world.

Ten

Kane didn't look in the mirror over his bathroom sink as he washed up. He focused instead on one task at a time. Wash his hands. Button up his shirt. Zip up his pants. Buckle his—ah, the belt was missing.

But he couldn't ignore the slight, almost imperceptible, shaking of his fingers.

He hadn't realized that, by encouraging Presley, he would unleash a tigress—not in a kinky way, but in the fierce way Presley made love. That intensity had reached a part of him Kane hadn't been prepared for her to touch.

I need a moment...just a moment more. The mantra was the only refrain in the stunned silence of his mind.

He would not think of Emily. Would not think about how this act, with this woman, far surpassed anything he had experienced before. How was that even possible?

I need a moment.

Far from ready, he stepped back into his bedroom, only to realize he might have been gone longer than he'd thought. Presley sat primly in the chair by the floor lamp, fully dressed. The small pool of light in the darkened room emphasized her isolation. At first glance, she looked exactly how she had when she'd come in here, but a closer look revealed the difference. The disheveled thickness of her hair. The slight twist at the waistband of her dress, giving it an off-kilter look. The shoes she had yet to slip onto her carefully placed feet.

"I need to go home."

The husky edge to her voice stirred him again, almost obliterating the actual words as he remembered her cries echoing in his ears. Then what she said truly registered.

Trying to keep things light, he asked, "Isn't that usually the man's line?"

Her eyes widened slightly, planting guilt in his heart for teasing her.

"I'm not really used to the protocol of these situations," she finally murmured.

Boy, he was an ass. But he'd been trying to ease her into being comfortable with their new, well, whatever this was. It certainly wasn't business. But it wasn't wholly pleasure, either, if their current strained conversation was any indication.

For a moment, Kane's fists clenched.

He hadn't intended things to go this far—though that was a lie if he thought long and hard about it. This woman held a unique attraction for him that he didn't understand and wasn't sure he was entirely comfortable with. In truth, he hadn't intended things to go this far *tonight*. But the sensations had quickly swept him away, like a river with category-four rapids.

He didn't realize he'd been staring until she reached up to smooth her hair back into place. When that didn't seem to work, she instinctively gathered it and put it back into its regular ponytail. Only she had no tie to hold it.

Without thought, he stepped to his chest of drawers. He took a ribbon from the valet box and extended it toward the woman who'd just rocked his world.

"Thank you," she murmured, then tied her hair back. She didn't ask where the ribbon was from.

Kane didn't offer.

Instead he knelt before her, resting his palms against her elbows. She had folded her arms over the front of her body, as if to protect herself from whatever came next. Her expression was carefully neutral. He could feel a slight tremble beneath his touch and wanted to smile. It reminded him of his own off-balance reaction just minutes earlier, but he kept his amusement to himself.

Instead he strove for a semiserious tone. "There isn't one particular protocol," he assured her. "Only whatever makes you the most comfortable."

Presley acknowledged him with a nod, but it was a few moments before she spoke. "I'm not really a stay-all-night kind of girl."

So why was he wishing she was? That she would spend the night in his arms and really reel him in?

Which was exactly what he didn't need. Shouldn't want. Yet he couldn't deny his strongest inclination.

Except in the face of her own needs.

He wasn't the sharpest tool in the shed, but Presley knew what she needed right now. Kane would give it to her.

Guiding her back downstairs, he bundled her up into her wrap once more. The silence between them on the drive to her family home wasn't comfortable—Presley fiddled, squirmed just a little—but Kane found himself reluctant to break it.

He simply couldn't shut down the thoughts whirling in his brain enough to make intelligent conversation.

Like a sneaky teenager, he turned off the SUV's lights and kept down any unnecessary noise as he approached the house. Somehow he knew Presley was too fragile for another confrontation with her stepmother. What she probably needed right now was simply to be alone.

Oddly enough, he didn't resent that. Even though he wanted the complete opposite.

He pulled right up to the side door, so she wouldn't have far to walk to get inside. He knew she'd be even quicker to slip out of the vehicle than normal.

He finally found his words when she stood just inside the open door, blinking in the glare of the cab lights as she gathered her sparkly clutch from the floor. He just couldn't let her go without telling her.

"Presley…"

She froze, her gaze caught in the intensity of his as

if she couldn't look away. He didn't want her to. She needed to see that he meant every word he said.

"Presley." He swallowed. "You were beautiful tonight. And I'm sure as hell not talking about your dress."

Kane stared at his hands gripping the steering wheel for long moments, shocked to realize he was second-guessing himself.

Normally, he'd never drop in on someone this early unannounced. But he knew enough about Presley to know she'd been up for a while and was probably already in the stables. Plus, this was a working racing establishment. More people than just Presley would be up and running.

This doubt was ridiculous.

He'd woken this morning with Presley on the brain—and his body had not been happy about his empty bed.

He was a grown man, unconcerned about appearing too eager. Besides, his interest would probably be the best thing for Presley to know. He'd made no mistake about wanting her, enjoying her, last night. He'd definitely like a repeat—a lot of repeats far into the future—regardless of contracts, agreements or money.

So get your ass out of the SUV and find her.

As soon as Kane opened the door, the sounds of early morning he'd heard every day of his adult life washed over him. Even though these weren't his stables, his horses, those sounds still brought peace, belonging and anticipation of a job he loved—no, not a job. A way of living.

Did Presley share those same feelings as she greeted her mornings?

Wow—philosophical Kane was getting damn touchy. Kane focused on the crunch of his boots on the gravel as he crossed to the already bustling barn. One of the hands on his way out held the door for him. The lowered light of the stables made Kane pause and blink to adjust.

Curious, he stepped to the stall that had been the focus of so much drama the other day and glanced inside.

The mare turned her head his way, curious about the new visitor. By way of greeting, he clicked his tongue softly; the sound caught her attention, and she neighed a quiet hello. This conversation of no words continued for several minutes before she deemed it safe enough to approach him.

"Hello, lovely girl," he crooned.

After a few strokes of her head and neck, she turned to nudge her lips against his palm.

"Sorry, girl. I came totally unprepared this morning."

That was probably an understatement. He had no idea what he would say to Presley, no idea what he would do. He'd simply woken with a need to be near her. So here he was.

"Ah, a cardinal sin when visiting the stables," Bennett said from his left. The stable manager stepped closer. "But then again, animals always think they're the reason you dropped by, so why wouldn't you bring a gift for them while you're at it."

He reached into his pocket and held a sugar cube out to Kane. They shared a grin, because they both knew

Bennett spoke the truth, then Kane fed the treat to the mare. No sooner had she lifted it delicately from his palm and crunched a few times before she returned to search for more. Kane shook his head as her searching lips tickled his palm.

"Sorry, girl." He turned to Bennett. "She doing okay? No ill effects?"

Appreciation flashed in Bennett's expression. "Doesn't seem like it. Her usual handler came back from vacation two days later, and that settled her down pretty good."

Kane nodded. "I'm glad."

"You here to see Presley?" Bennett asked.

"If she's not busy."

"She's always busy, but if you're willing to wait her out, you might get somewhere." He gestured toward the inner recesses of the building. "I'll show you where to find her."

Kane steeled himself for any awkwardness. Her virtual sprint from his place last night concerned him. Knowing Presley, she'd probably done some second-guessing herself this morning—hell, all night—and he wanted to put her at ease.

Bennett took a left turn at the large cross aisle Kane remembered from before, then headed down to the open double doors at the end. Stepping back out into the bright morning sunlight left Kane blinking for a moment, then he noticed he was on the side of the stables where several training paddocks were set up. The white-painted railings looked neat and in good repair.

"Presley is down in the far paddock, where the jumps are set up."

A flash of heat engulfed Kane. His stomach turned. "Jumps?"

Bennett nodded. "She's working with a new horse, training him for shows for a client."

No matter how harshly Kane told himself this was a common activity for any horse owner, he could not bar the images that flooded his brain. Emily preparing herself and her horse for the approaching jump. Emily's eyes going wide the minute she realized something was very wrong. Emily's body twisting as she hit the hard ground in an unnatural position.

He sucked in a breath, drawing Bennett's attention. "You okay, Kane?"

From somewhere beyond his boiling emotions, Kane dug out a smile and a "sure thing."

Bennett seemed to buy it. "I'll let you walk on down, if you don't mind. I need to head back in."

Kane thought he said, "No problem," but he honestly wasn't sure. Bennett smiled, waved and went back the way they'd come, so Kane's response must have been adequate. He stood where he was, braced against the storm inside him, afraid the minute he relaxed he would either collapse or lose the contents of his stomach. And he wouldn't be able to explain away either.

He tried to think logically but couldn't at the moment. So he stood baking in the heat—outside and in his head—just trying to survive the next few minutes.

He could see the horse and rider making rounds in the paddock. Warming up, maybe? The jumps weren't that high. It was a standard early training setup. People jumped horses and went to competitions all the time. Kane had even attended a few since the accident and experienced no discomfort whatsoever. So why did he still feel like he was going to puke up the breakfast he'd wolfed down?

The horse paused, Presley holding him at rest. Would she be able to tell Kane was here if she looked this way? Suddenly the steel traps on his legs loosened. He walked to a nearby stand of trees, but the shade didn't give him any relief.

At least, not that he noticed.

The horse started forward again. *She's fine. Everything's fine.* The mantra didn't help. The approach to the first low jump was flawless, but Kane didn't stick around for the execution.

He didn't remember the walk back to his SUV. Didn't even remember much of the drive. He only remembered the grip of his hands around the steering wheel as the SUV took him as far away from Presley as possible.

Eleven

"So what did you do to ruin this relationship? Or are you the only woman in history who could make a deal that was purely business with that man?"

Presley stared at Marjorie, startled for a moment to have her own fears spoken out loud. "What?"

"Well, he hasn't been here since the party the other night. Maybe he's just tired of having to defend you everywhere he goes."

Her stepmother had been more than a little irritable since Kane's rebuke the other night. Presley had hoped she would get over it, but she'd apparently decided instead to take her ire out on Presley.

"Everything's fine. I'm sure he's just busy."

"So it *is* solely business."

Presley's cheeks started to burn as memories of their

one night together rose in her mind. She did her best to push them away. The last thing she wanted was to think about that while Marjorie watched her for any clue as to what was really happening between her and Kane.

She hadn't talked to Marjorie about sex, even during puberty. She had no intention of starting now.

"I forgot something in the barn."

She turned on her heel, but Marjorie continued to speak behind her. "Presley, you come back here and tell me what's going on right now."

So you can tell all your friends and they can all smile sympathetically every time I walk into a room for the next six months?

Presley kept right on walking, all the way to her truck.

It had been three days since Kane had dropped her off that night. She hadn't expected him to rush right over, but a phone call, maybe…a text, even… Some acknowledgment of what had happened between them.

Nothing. Not a single word in three days. And call her old-fashioned, but an innately feminine part of her wanted Kane to make the first move. Somehow prove to her that he was still interested.

It looked as though she wasn't going to get her wish.

But they still had a contract, and as uncomfortable as this meeting might be, Presley needed to know if the deal was still on…or if she was going have to find the funds to pay the Harringtons what Marjorie owed in full. That could be a purely business conversation, right?

She was still wondering how the heck she would

pull that off when she drove her truck into the circular driveway of his house in town. Part of her wondered if he would even be here. But it was the end of the day, and she'd figured there was a fifty-fifty chance that he'd finished his work at the Harrington stables. His SUV by the garage told her she'd guessed right.

As she climbed the front steps, the clip of her boots on the stone reminded her she was still in her work clothes. Great. She was just reinforcing the image of not being good enough, with dirty clothes and muddy boots and hay in her hair. This plan might have been poorly thought out.

But this was her. He could take it or leave it.

The thought brought a smirk to her lips, and she forced herself onward. Kane might not be interested in her as a bed partner after having tasted her once, but that didn't mean they couldn't still be business partners. She'd spent three days wondering if he'd renege on his contract. It was time to put the doubts to rest.

Kane didn't look surprised when he opened the door. Presley only hoped her expression was giving away as little as his. He didn't speak, simply stepped back and motioned her inside. *Not very promising.*

She stomped over the threshold but quickly caught herself once she realized what she was doing. Neither leaving a trail of tiny dirt clumps nor walking like a three-year-old having a tantrum would reflect well on her. But the more her nerves jangled, the more anger crept in.

Turning to face him across the foyer, she noticed that she'd crossed her arms over her middle but allowed herself the defensive gesture. She needed comfort, to say the least, as she jumped right in.

"Wanna tell me what's going on, Kane?"

"Hey, Presley."

His even response as he closed the door threatened to wiggle through all the defenses she was building. She did her best not to read anything into it as he gestured her into the living room. She got a quick impression of leather furniture complimenting the dark wood floors before she turned her focus back on him.

She refused to soften her tone as she asked, "Have you been okay, Kane? Sick?"

"No," he said with a shake of his head. "I wish I had that kind of excuse. But we both know I don't."

"I don't know anything. Care to enlighten me?"

Instead of giving her an excuse, any excuse, he started to pace. His own boots beat out a tattoo across the floorboards. The view of his strong back and tight rear made her mouth water. But the scowl on his face when he turned around was enough to make her look away.

Her heartbeat picked up speed like a train leaving the station. She had to face the fact that this wasn't about business, as much as she might wish it was. No, this was personal. Very personal.

Her arms squeezed even tighter over her chest, only giving the illusion of security. She averted her gaze, looking off toward the doorway, no longer able to handle Kane and his silence.

"I'm sorry, Kane," she finally said. "I'm sorry if you were disappointed the other night."

Her quiet words landed like a firecracker in the room. Kane jerked to a halt, finally showing one emotion. Shock. And something else, something darker that she couldn't make out.

He shook his head a few times. "Are we remembering the same night?" he asked. "Because from my viewpoint that isn't even an issue."

Presley blinked. How was that possible after the way he behaved? "Look, I'm used to guys not calling, so you don't have to feel bad. But I'm not usually under contract with them, so..."

"Not usually?" Kane asked, his brow rising.

How could one look make her feel like such a ditz? "Okay, never. Which is why we need to get this, um, figured out."

There, that was pretty close to businesslike.

But Kane still didn't answer. He squeezed his eyes closed and rubbed his hand against the back of his neck. Presley waited while her stomach churned, her mind tumbling through the possibilities of what he would say next.

Patience had never been her strong suit. "I just don't want anything that happened between us personally to affect our contract. What we expect from each other."

"Why would it?"

Was he really this dense? Or just being difficult?

"I don't know, Kane," she suddenly exploded. Her breath came hard and fast as her emotions outstripped her control. "I have no idea why you're suddenly being an inconsiderate jerk, okay?"

She swallowed hard, but the feelings refused to be

locked back up inside. Turning around, she rushed for the doorway, intent only on getting out of there before she did something stupid—like bursting into tears.

A firm grip on her arm whirled her back around. In seconds Kane was hard against her with the wall at her back. And all her anger detonated into a white-hot passion inside her.

His lips met hers as if he felt it, too. No polite inquiry or gentleness here. He insisted she open for him, then conquered every inch of the territory within. Need spiked as his tongue met hers.

He pressed closer, his hips grinding against her. If she'd thought their one night together was all they had, his body told a whole different story. Her groans echoed in her ears. She clutched at his arms, desperation shoving aside everything but desire. Kane reluctantly pulled away from her lips, only to dive for the vulnerable length of her neck.

His ragged breathing hitched as he nuzzled, suckled and nipped at her skin. Presley rose on her toes, eager for more.

Luckily Kane didn't settle. His hands fumbled at her shirt, jerking it from her waistband, then up over her head.

She didn't have time to think about bare skin in daylight or what bra she had on. Kane stripped her of it soon enough.

His hands kneading her breasts made everything in her tighten, her body aching for Kane's rough passion.

Her nipples tingled in anticipation and were rewarded when Kane drew first one, then the other into his mouth. Presley's head fell back against the wall, her hands buried in Kane's hair.

Only in these moments could she forget her own hang-ups and just let herself feel.

With a grunt, Kane's hands moved to the button on her jeans. Relief flooded through her when he finally got the fly open and started to wriggle them down her hips.

She wanted to cry when he paused. Then he stepped back, allowing cool air to drift over her skin. He glanced down, then back up to meet her wide-eyed gaze.

To her pride, he looked a little dazed as he gave her a half grin. "I don't think this is gonna work," he murmured.

"What?" Her question was slightly slurred.

Kane glanced back down. So did she—only to see their boots.

Yep. That would make getting out of her pants a bit of a challenge.

Instead of stepping away or letting her go, Kane pressed close once more. He spoke against her ear, reviving the goose bumps across her skin. "If I haven't made myself clear, I have no problem with you or what happened the other night. Got it?"

"Then why the hell didn't you call?" she mumbled.

"We'll get to that. Just don't ever think that I don't want you, Presley. Ever."

Seriously? She found herself pushing him back, even though the move exposed far more than she was comfortable with. "What else am I supposed to think, Kane? It's been three days. Three days without a word."

In true male fashion, Kane glanced down but then met her gaze once more. "That's because I'm a jerk. Nothing to do with you. Got it?"

She shook her head. Because she didn't get it. She didn't understand. "That's not good enough. Tell me why."

He took a deep breath, then turned away. "That's a very good question."

Kane didn't look back as he heard Presley scramble for her clothes. The least he could do was give her a chance to make herself decent after he'd almost stripped her bare.

The pull was strong, the desire to return to the heat of her skin and the eager passion she gave him when he touched her.

But he couldn't. Not now.

Just the thought of what he had to tell her killed the desire racing through his body like a fire extinguisher putting out a flame. But if he wanted to undo the damage he'd inflicted on Presley, on her self-esteem, he had to own up to why he'd stayed away. She deserved his honesty.

Which totally sucked.

Kane didn't like talking about Emily. He didn't even talk about her with Mason, who'd been there through every stage of the relationship. Discovery, bliss, tragedy and absolute rejection. Could Kane make his actions toward Presley understood without having to reveal all the nitty-gritty details about Emily?

He hoped so.

Finally the sounds behind him stopped. Kane turned to face his punishment. "I did come by, actually."

Presley tilted her head to the side, wisps of hair that had come loose from her inevitable ponytail dancing around her head. "What? When?"

"The next morning."

He could see her try to think back, probably searching for what she'd done that morning and how it could have run him off. There was no point in speculating, but she didn't know that yet.

"Bennett led me through the stables out to the paddock where you were training."

Recognition dawned in those pretty green eyes, but no understanding. *He* didn't even understand his extreme reaction himself.

"You were working on jumps and I—" Kane paused as his throat closed. In his mind, he cursed. Why the hell couldn't he keep it together?

"Yes," she said slowly. "Black Jack's just started."

The jumps were low. There was nothing dangerous about what she'd been doing. Nothing upsetting. He could almost hear her think, *what's the big deal?*

"I was engaged once."

His words sounded too loud in the room, as if they echoed off the hardwood floors and walls. Her green eyes flared. She sucked in a deep breath. "I know."

"You knew that?" he asked, delaying the inevitable.

Her nod was cautious. "I just heard Mason mention that you'd had a fiancée the other night. That's it."

"What kind of lover are you?" he asked, trying to lighten the mood. "Not even a single internet search?"

Her cheeks turned a delicate pink that entranced him. "Well, I didn't have much to go on."

At least she was honest. "I wouldn't have blamed you if you had. But anyway…" Where should he start? How much should he say? "It was a few years ago and we were together—" More years than he cared to remember.

"She was an accomplished rider. We had big plans. Emily loved horses as much as I did."

A movement brought his gaze back to Presley, even though he hadn't realized he'd looked away. Tentative steps brought her closer, though her arms were still wrapped around her waist. She hadn't bothered to tuck in her shirt, but everything else seemed to be in place.

"We were at a competition when it happened. Something went wrong with the jump. I'm still not sure what. It surprised her, too, and she couldn't recover properly."

"Oh, Kane," Presley said, shaking her head as if in denial. She'd been around animals long enough she probably didn't need more details. Just the important one. "But she lived?"

He nodded. "Permanently paralyzed from the waist down."

Ignoring Presley's gasp, he forced himself to go on. "But she no longer wanted anything to do with me or the dreams we had together. She moved to a city where she never had to see another horse. Got a job. Married a man. Built a new life. And I don't blame her one bit."

Liar.

"So my jumping upset you?" Presley asked, confusion in her tone.

"I don't know why," Kane said with a shrug. "I'm around animals a lot. Been to plenty of competitions since then. Shouldn't be a problem." He met her gaze head on. "Won't be a problem."

She wanted to say something. He could tell. But she shook her head, then suddenly changed tack. "So we're good?" she asked.

Kane switched gears immediately, grateful to leave the subject of his stupid behavior and broken engagement far behind. He stalked toward her, enjoying the sensation of control as her eyes widened. "No."

Presley blinked. "No?"

"I think it's a little soon to be good."

She wasn't following, so he gave her a demonstration. First he swooped her up into his arms, then dropped her onto the leather couch. Her cry quickly turned into a giggle. Then she gasped as he straddled one of her legs, bringing his thigh high between hers. "Kane," she said, breathless, "I came straight from the stables. I'm dirty."

He leaned in close, bracing his palms on the smooth surface on each side of her head. The urge to imprint himself on her was overwhelming, but he maintained just a few inches of distance. "Let's get this straight," he said, bending his elbows so he could bring his mouth to her skin. "I spend regular parts of my day getting sweaty and dirty."

He grinned as she sighed from the sensations of having him this close.

"I find you fascinating, Presley. I told you before, it's not about the dress."

His hips dipped briefly to press into the cradle of hers. "I like you messy. I like you clean. I like you fancy. I'll take you however I can get you."

"Yes," she moaned, arching to press his lips harder against her.

He nibbled his way up to her earlobe. After giving the soft flesh a firm nip, he whispered in her ear. "And right now, I have only one thing on my mind."

"What's that?"

"Getting you out of these boots."

Twelve

"Are you using this trip to force me to stay the night?" Presley asked as she looked around their elaborate suite in the boutique hotel Kane had chosen in Louisville.

The question was a little tongue in cheek, but her nerves were very real. This would be her first night to stay in Kane's arms. Her first time to wake up with him. Was she crazy?

To hide the jitteriness invading her limbs, she strode over to the balcony doors. Each room had its own individual balcony with side walls made of wrought-iron covered in clinging ivy. Gorgeous.

"Hey, whatever works," Kane said from directly behind her.

With a natural ease that still discomfited her, Kane slipped his arms around her and pressed his lips against her temple. Affection came as naturally to him as sex—something she hadn't expected.

"Men are devious about getting their way," he added, amusement in his voice.

And for some reason, this was something he wanted. Not in a pushy way, but he'd asked her every night they were together to stay. She never did. There were no demands, no fuss. But the question came like clockwork.

"What devious men want is rarely the best for everyone involved," she quipped, then automatically wished she could take the words back. They were too revealing for her comfort.

Her instincts told her that sleeping beside him all night would be the end of her ability to stay detached. Thus the nerves that had her eyeing the king-size bed with something akin to fear, mixed with an excitement she couldn't deny.

Honestly, was her current state really, truly detached? No...but it was comforting to delude herself.

When he wrapped his arms around her, it chipped away at her resolve, as did his low whistle when she came out of the dressing room a little later. She was wearing the very dress that had made her stare into the dressing room mirror weeks ago. The deep jewel-blue, silky material, and flowing length made her feel special, especially when Kane complimented her. Every sexy, whispered word of praise made her ache to dive in headfirst and not think about later. Why did she have to be such a practical kind of girl?

She tried to put practicalities aside and enjoy the luxury of the limo that took them to their first event in

Louisville—the annual dinner put on by the American Horse Racing Society to kick off the festivities leading up to the Kentucky Derby race.

She savored his hand at the small of her back. The assurance that this dress— her breakthrough dress, she often called it —actually looked and felt good on her.

As the dinner got into full swing, she tried to loosen up enough to consider tonight magical, even if the thought made her practical, party-hating self choke a little on her champagne.

To her surprise, it was magical for a couple of hours. With Kane at her side, they chatted with her friends whom he'd already met. She introduced him around to acquaintances in the business. They even sat with Justine Simone during the meal.

But the magic ended the minute she stepped out of a stall in the ladies' room to find Joan applying lipstick at the mirror.

"Oh," Presley said, "I didn't even realize you were here."

Judging from the frown that appeared on the other woman's face, that wasn't the right choice of words.

"I'm not surprised," Joan said with an exasperated drawl.

"Um, excuse me?"

"Mooning like a cow is not becoming—or ladylike. But we both know that's not one of your strong suits."

Presley stood for a moment, perplexed. Joan hadn't been this direct in her attacks since they were teenagers. Teenage girls weren't subtle; they didn't hold anything back. Oddly, the words didn't upset Presley, but only confused her.

Her body made up her mind for her, and she automatically moved forward to wash her hands. Whatever was stuck in Joan's craw would just have to stay there. Presley wasn't in the mood.

Ignoring the woman watching her, she carefully straightened her dress, making sure no part of it had gotten tucked into her underwear by accident. Then she reached into the little clutch she carried and retrieved a new lip gloss—praying the whole time someone else would come in and break up the tension.

No such luck.

As Joan continued to stare, a flush of anger ignited in Presley's core. Joan and her like had always made Presley feel ashamed, as though she were less than them. Not today. Somehow her self-esteem had gotten Kane's message.

Apparently her application of the lip gloss was the catalyst to break Joan's silence.

"Makeup? Really, Presley?" Joan shifted to rest against the counter as if taking up a front row seat. "The girl who has always gone au naturel is wearing makeup for a man?"

Presley studied the mirror. Most women wouldn't even consider what she wore now as true makeup. Some powder, lip gloss and eye shadow, applied using the very basic technique she'd managed to master. That was all. She smiled, watching her barely red lips move in the mirror. But beneath the smile was something very, very different.

"And that dress," Joan continued. "Are you seriously attracting a man with that?"

"Everyone else likes it."

"They're just being polite."

Kane picked it out.

Joan wasn't finished. "It's embarrassing how hard you're trying—only to fail so publicly."

Presley watched her own brows rise in the mirror, as if her reflection were questioning this new accusation. "Fail?" Presley could only be proud that her tone and expression were calm, since her insides were anything but.

Joan shook her head from side to side, as if in pity. "Kane could have simply paid you for your expertise, if that's what he was after. It seems to be the only thing other men want from you. But he is a man, after all... They're gonna take what's on offer, if it's free."

Presley's breath caught hard in her chest.

"Until something better comes along," Joan added with an arch smile.

I don't think so. "And that something is you?"

The fake shock Joan adopted wasn't fooling Presley. "Well," Joan said, drawing the word out as if she were reluctant to continue, "I don't see why not."

"Right. Because you have so much to offer, I guess?"

Now Joan turned to the mirror to straighten her own dress. The preening nauseated Presley.

"Honestly, I don't see much on offer besides a pretty face and stylish clothes. The problem is there's not a single original thought in your head."

"What?" Joan gasped, her expression more shocked

than it should be. She probably hadn't been prepared for Presley to fight back.

"I didn't stutter," Presley said, her tone only a little shaky.

"Look here, you—"

Presley stepped forward. "No, you listen." She straightened her posture a notch, using her extra inch over Joan to her advantage. "I've put up with a lot over the years. I've ignored, pouted and, yes, even cried a few times."

She pressed a little closer, which caused Joan's eyes to widen.

"But we aren't children anymore, Joan. And I don't have to put up with the manure you're shoveling. Do not talk to me again, or I will not hesitate to make your life as miserable as you've made mine in the past."

Presley didn't wait for an answer. She swung toward the exit and kept walking. Only when she'd pulled back the door did Joan shout, "You won't win."

"I already have."

"He won't stay long."

This time, Presley looked back, giving Joan her full attention. "See, that's how silly you are. That doesn't matter. This isn't about Kane."

"Yes—"

"It's about you and me, Joan. And at the end of the day, you still have to live with yourself. But I don't." She stepped forward, letting the door go so it could slowly swing shut. But the last word was still hers as she caught Kane's gaze on her from a few feet away. "So, yeah, I win."

* * *

Kane smiled slightly at Presley's words, though they obviously weren't spoken to him. The door to the ladies' room slid silently shut as she walked straight to him and took his arm, her expression calm and almost triumphant. He glanced back over her shoulder, catching a glimpse of Joan storming out the door to glare at them.

Or, rather, Presley.

But she never looked back, and Kane was damn proud of her. He didn't know what had transpired in there, but Presley had obviously come out on top. He took a couple of steps to meet her.

"Did you put someone in her place?" he murmured.

Presley paused in her forward push and blinked at him. He could see her register her surroundings for the first time.

He couldn't help but tease. "Well, she seemed to have all her hair. You must not have tried hard enough."

That brought her up short. "I wouldn't resort to hair pulling."

Kane grinned. "Sometimes they deserve it."

"I'm fine just using words," she said, but she did match his smile with a sheepish version of her own.

"That's my girl. Let's go."

"Already?" she asked.

He bent close to her ear as he took her arm. "You deserve a reward."

But as he turned toward the door, their plans were interrupted.

"Great to see you again, young lady," the man Kane

had been speaking with said as Presley came so close she almost settled against him.

"Mr. Stephens," she exclaimed, moving away long enough to give the graying man a hug. "I didn't see you earlier."

"Oh, we arrived a bit late," the man said. "A little car trouble on the way, but we finally made it."

"That's good. Kane, have you met Mr. Stephens? He was my original trainer, but has been a friend of the family for many, many years."

"Oh, yes," Stephens said as he shook Kane's hand. "So wonderful to meet the newest celebrity in our little club."

Kane watched as the two shared a look that spoke volumes he wasn't privy to—and found himself surprised by the sudden questions peppering his brain.

"So how's the training going?" Mr. Stephens asked Presley. "That new young'un getting a hang of things?"

A cold sensation seeped into Kane's chest. He knew exactly what kind of training Stephens was referring to.

"Yes," she said, enthusiasm coloring her voice. "Just a little more work and I think we will lick that hitch. Once he gets some maturity on him, he'll be a champion jumper. Your jockey will be thrilled."

Stephens turned to Kane with a beaming glow. "She's one of the best students I ever worked with. All those trophies aren't just for show."

Kane forced a smile, though his feelings were already in deep freeze. He'd gone out of his way not to mention Presley's jumping practices again. Sometimes he could almost convince himself that they didn't happen. And he was okay with that, for now. After all, he wasn't delusional enough to think the issue wouldn't come up at some point...far in the future.

They talked about the gelding's finer points and what Presley was doing to correct his approach. Kane let the words swirl around him, let the confusion and re-membered pain melt away as they moved on to other subjects, let himself admire the confident woman who stood by his side.

By the time they left Stephens, Kane was more than ready to cut their evening short. Presley didn't pro-test as he led her to the lobby and called for the limo. They'd barely made it inside before Kane took her lips with his, an unmistakable need rising like a tide inside him. However long he had her, he would make it the best time they'd ever had.

Her lips were soft, but the grip of her hands was strong. She pulled him closer, her eagerness leaving him gasping. The dark taste of the wine she'd drunk at the party and the delicate smell of honeysuckle in-toxicated him.

He buried his face in the crook of her neck, breath-ing deep, then licked along the ridge of her collarbone, taking in her flavor. Her gasps played on the air like music. Kane pulled her close, struggling for control. How much longer was it to the hotel?

He was proud he didn't drag her through the lobby to the elevator at high speed. The instinct was there, but he controlled himself. Barely. No need to spoil the surprise.

They came through the door to a darkened room, only a couple of lamps casting a dim glow. Her shy smile as he led her to the balcony doors intrigued him, urged him to push this further than she might be comfortable with.

He led her through the door the staff had left open to find the soft glow of electric candles on the small table outside. The ivy created a sense of a walled-in space, isolating them from the city around them, darkening the area to a level of intimacy that heightened Kane's senses.

Presley stepped toward the table for two. "What's this?" she asked, surprise lightening her tone.

Kane didn't even have to look. More champagne. Slices of decadent coconut cake. "Your favorite," he said simply.

She glanced back at him, but he couldn't make out her expression in the dark. When she spoke, her voice had grown husky. "What if I had eaten dessert already?"

"You didn't," he said, stepping closer. "Chocolate cake doesn't seem to appeal to you."

"You noticed?"

"I notice everything about you, Presley." *Even the things I don't want to see because they worry me.*

He lifted a bite to her lips, the candlelight glinting off the silver fork. Over and over he fed her, appeasing her hunger more important to him than feeding his own.

"You're spoiling me," she murmured between bites.

"Good. Someone should."

Suddenly the night flared to life, sparkling lights and the popping of fireworks filling the sky. Presley turned to look, giving Kane a brief glimpse of her profile. He switched the candles off and led Presley to the rail, abandoning their dessert. She gripped the support, face lifted for the famous fireworks show preceding the Kentucky Derby.

Kane was much more interested in creating some fireworks of their own.

The thickness of her hair as he pulled it to the side made him anticipate seeing it spread across a pillow in the early hours of the morning. He tasted the light sheen of salt on her skin as he kissed the back of her neck. He stood close enough to feel the shiver that traveled down her spine at his touch.

It was more intoxicating than the champagne. Hell, it was more intoxicating than a good bottle of scotch.

He sucked lightly, moving to the sensitive junction where her neck met her shoulders. She arched back into him. Her softness molding to his hardness made him groan. He heard a slight huff of air, as if she were smothering a laugh, and decided he'd be happy to make her pay for her amusement.

Pressing closer, he used his body to bend her toward the rail. She didn't protest. Her breath sped up as his hands found her hips. Slow and sure, he let his palms follow the silky-soft material down the outsides of her thighs. Then he bunched it up so he could slip beneath the hem and indulge his desire to feel skin against skin.

"What are you doing?" she murmured, turning to watch him over her shoulder. Her voice only conveyed a hint of dismay, far less than what he'd been expecting.

He couldn't help but chuckle. "What do you think?" He lifted back up to align his body close against hers, whispering in her ear. "Trust me."

* * *

Trust me?

Presley wasn't so sure about that, but Kane's touch convinced her to leave the worry to him. Though she knew no one could see them, her brain automatically equated outside with being in public, Kane didn't seem to care.

Pretty soon, his mouth and hands convinced her she didn't care, either.

She tried to breathe, tried to hold on to her sanity, but it simply wasn't happening. His hands roamed her thighs, massaging the muscles in a way that made her want to turn into jelly. Her heels made her the perfect height, so she fit neatly against his body. He was aroused. He wanted her.

And she wanted this.

She didn't protest when she felt the cool night air against the backs of her thighs. The front of her dress still fell straight from her waist, which calmed her irrational fears of being seen. His hands briefly clasped her hips, as if positioning her for his pleasure. She had to press her lips together to hold back the moan that ached to escape.

The fireworks continued in the distance, but Presley hardly even saw them. Her focus turned inward to the need buffeting her body. Behind her she heard the rasp of a zipper, the rustle of clothing, the rip of the little foil packet.

Kane nudged the inside of her ankle, spreading her legs a little wider, leaving her exposed. One of his hands meandered around the front, sliding beneath the scrap of lace between her thighs. The throb of her core deepened. She panted through the need to beg.

Back and forth his fingers played, leaving her aching and wet. Without thought, she shifted, tilting herself back in invitation. Taking advantage, Kane fitted himself against her and slid home. Everything inside Presley tightened, desperate to keep him with her.

"Yes," he hissed, giving her little nub a flick with his fingers as a reward.

This time she couldn't cut her cry off before it escaped. It was followed quickly by Kane's groan of satisfaction. Ever so slowly, he withdrew. Then he returned at the same pace, allowing her to feel every inch of delicious fullness. She expected him to pick up the pace, but he didn't. For what seemed like an eternity, he played with her. The push forward filled her and also bumped her against his hand. The increase in pressure sent ecstasy coursing along her nerves, but never quite enough to send her over the edge.

The pullback shot her need higher, the glide eliciting a whimper just short of begging. But Kane wasn't in the mood to hurry, it seemed. Instead of speed, he added force, taking her up on her toes with each thrust. She tracked his climb by the harsh tempo of his breath with the intimate recognition only a lover would have—a fact that added to her awe.

Then all thought was lost. Waves of pleasure rolled over her body, crashing deep inside just as the crescendo of fireworks exploded before her eyes. Her cry was lost in the roar of the explosion and the distant applause of the crowd across the city. One thrust, two, then Kane joined her, pressing himself deep inside her and holding hard as his body gained release. She soaked in his groan, the tight grip of his hands.

As she stared out into the night, she knew that everything had changed. *She* had changed. The barriers were gone, leaving her heart exposed. It was his for the taking.

She had a feeling she'd never get it back.

Thirteen

Presley walked through the beginning half of Derby Day feeling off kilter, as if she were on a cruise and couldn't find her sea legs.

It wasn't a physical sensation, though. Her body moved with a languid ease that she'd never experienced before but could definitely attribute to Kane's TLC. If last night hadn't been satisfying enough, the way he'd woken her up this morning definitely finished the job.

She'd thought she was dreaming as dawn crept into the room. A slow coming to consciousness prompted by the smooth glide of warm skin against her own. Kane's leisurely, silent loving this morning, being surrounded by his scent, only made her crave him more. His touch had lit a fire inside her that pushed all sleepiness aside, replacing it with white-hot need. A need Kane had more than met.

No, the problem this morning was definitely a mental game.

She'd been afraid to stay with Kane overnight, and her fears had been justified. Despite knowing this was a business arrangement, she'd managed to fall hook, line and sinker for the gentleman behind the contract. A man who seemed to have no interest in making this a long-term arrangement.

He was kind, attentive, sexy—and completely close-mouthed about anything to do with his emotions or history beyond business. He'd never again mentioned his ex-fiancée, nor Presley's training pursuits, even though she secretly wished his comments meant he was interested in her personally.

No such luck. The only true depth of emotion they experienced was in bed.

"Mint julep, ma'am?" a meandering waiter asked, balancing his tray of gorgeous cut-glass tumblers. Though it wasn't even noon, she eagerly reached for one, hoping it might calm her nerves. She sipped the signature concoction while she and Kane waited for lunch to be served in Millionaires Row.

Kane eyed her drink, then let his gaze drift over the sea of hats and fancy clothes surrounding them. "Pretty impressive," he murmured.

So was he. The white suit and pale purple shirt and tie set off his dark good looks in a mouthwatering way.

"You've never been here for Derby Day?" she asked instead of giving voice to her appreciative thoughts.

"Definitely not like this," he said, surveying the room a second time.

The announcement that lunch was about to be served produced a surge of three hundred guests toward the doors to the dining area. Kane took her arm.

"I've only witnessed the race in person once, though we watched it every year on television," he continued as they headed in to lunch. "My father brought us here the year after my mother died. We were in the infield with a picnic from a fast food chicken place. But we each got brand-new dress clothes for the occasion and stayed in a run-down motel across town—the only rooms available that Dad could afford."

His smile took Presley's breath away as he went on. "We didn't care. We were at the derby. I remember every moment of that weekend."

Presley swallowed hard against the lump in her throat. "You're amazing, you know?"

Kane settled her into her seat, then pulled his own chair out. He removed his suit jacket and sat down beside her. As their dining table slowly filled, he leaned close, so their heads were almost touching. "How so?"

"It takes a special kind of person not to be resentful of that, heck, of everything that happened to your family," she said, holding his dark gaze for the first time today.

Kane smirked, though the look in his eyes remained somber. "I think Mason has proven that revenge only backfires."

Presley thought back to the rumors surrounding Mason and EvaMarie's reunion romance. "Guess so."

Kane frowned at his water glass. "There are still times I don't understand why my father did what he did. Why didn't he use the money from my mother to make life easier on himself?"

"Did he ever give you a reason?"

Kane's smirk grew into a grin. "Besides honoring my mother's wish that the money be used for us boys? His only other answer was pride."

Presley lowered her voice as the seats around them filled. "What? Why?"

Kane leaned a little closer. "Since he moved back to her hometown to finish raising us, he didn't want her parents and people in that town accusing him of being a gold digger, just as they had when he'd married her. He knew that if he suddenly had money to spare, they'd gossip, and that gossip would eventually get back to Mason and me."

Kane absently fingered one of the loose strands of her hair. She knew he loved it down, so today she'd worn it with just a simple turquoise fascinator with feathers and ribbon pinned to one side, instead of the traditional hat worn by most of the ladies in attendance.

"I'm sure he would have withdrawn some funds if he'd needed it to feed us," Kane continued, "but once he was working again, our situation wasn't dire. Things became easier, and he really just left the money where it was and forgot about it for long periods of time."

Flash. Flash.

Presley squinted as an unexpected flare of light surprised her. She glanced across the table as Kane turned in the direction of the light. A grinning man with a camera covering half his face snapped another picture. Presley eased closer to Kane as a wave of unease swept through her.

"Gorgeous couple," the man said as he lowered the camera. "Bernie with the *Louisville Scene*."

He strode around the table to shake Kane's hand. "I recognized you right away, Mr. Harrington. I've been following the opening of the Harrington stables since the big announcement a couple of months ago."

"That's very flattering," Kane said.

"News isn't what gets hits anymore," Bernie said. "In this digital era, we've gotta reel 'em in, and stories like yours are just the ticket. Working man turned billionaire overnight. Who wouldn't want to see themselves in that story?"

Presley noticed the other occupants of their table blatantly watching and listening to the overeager photographer. She felt herself blushing.

"Let's get a few more of you with your lovely date. What's your name, sweetheart?"

Kane glanced her way, his smile stiff this time. "Presley?"

"Yes?"

It took a moment before she noticed his gaze pointedly slip from hers to her hand curved around his upper arm. Her fingernails were digging into the fabric of his shirt. She immediately released him and drew in a subtle breath. It was as if the muscles in her hand had stiffened into a permanent position, but after a few seconds of concentration, she was able to relax them.

"Presley?" Bernie's voice boomed loud enough now to catch the attention of people at other tables in their general vicinity. "That's an unusual name. I've only known one woman with that name, and I seriously wanted to give that woman the name of a beauty consultant. Sad, really."

As he grinned at her expectantly, Presley wanted to crawl under the table and disappear.

Kane stood, holding his hand out to her. As much as she didn't want her picture splattered all over the internet, maybe if they got this over with quickly, the photographer would go bother someone else. To her surprise, Kane unobtrusively positioned her at his side, using a heavy palm against her back. Then he reached around and flipped her hair forward over her shoulder before briefly catching her chin with his fingers.

"Just smile pretty," he murmured.

A few flashes later and Presley wanted to collapse back into her seat, feeling like a baby for making a big deal out of nothing. But the churning of her stomach and burning of her cheeks took a while to subside.

Kane shook the man's hand again, and Bernie turned to go. *Free!* But she had a sinking feeling she'd celebrated too soon as he pivoted back toward them after a few steps.

"Miss, I didn't get your full name for the caption," he said, smiling in a way that should have set her at ease, but didn't.

"Presley Macarthur," Kane supplied.

Bernie paused, his pen hovering over his little note-book, staring at her with his mouth agape. "No. You can't be Presley Macarthur."

Presley braced herself for what she could see coming. Not an apology for what he'd said earlier. Only more insults. "Why not?"

"You don't look anything like her—um, yourself." He glanced up and down, studying her as if trying to find something. "I mean, I've seen her—you—at lots of races. You look beautiful. Before you were…"

"Careful." Kane's voice had gone guttural.

Bernie glanced at him with wide eyes. "Right. Must be going. Lots of people to get on camera."

Kane shifted as if to return to the table, but Presley couldn't move. He stepped close for a moment. "Just ignore him," he said, solely for her ears.

Luckily the noise level in the room was higher now that the tables were full of hungry partygoers. It gave Presley a sense of protection, of privacy.

Still she found herself staring blankly over Kane's shoulder. "Do you think everyone is talking about me like that?"

She didn't want to sound like a whiny child seek-ing attention, but she was very afraid that was how she came off. Except it hadn't occurred to her that the changes she'd made would put her at the mercy of peo-ple like Bernie, people she felt compelled to be polite to, even though they didn't play by the same rules.

Once more Kane nudged her chin with his fingers until she looked up to meet his gaze. "If they can't see how beautiful you are, how beautiful, smart and talented you've always been…you don't need 'em."

And she didn't. But she was afraid she might need Kane for a long, long time to come.

After the whirlwind of derby weekend, Kane desperately wanted to relax. He didn't mind people. But there was too much of a good thing. His body needed rest; his eyes needed tranquil green; his ears needed nature.

He knew Presley felt the same. Just remembering her face when the photographer had questioned her made Kane ache. By the end of the weekend, she'd been more than anxious to get home.

So much for spending the night.

Such a strong woman shouldn't be made to feel low by a reporter's thoughtless words. While Kane was glad he'd helped her show her true beauty to the world, he understood better now why she'd never taken that step on her own.

He'd watched the *Louisville Scene* website to make sure no derogatory remarks were posted. Though the pictures did appear and correctly identified them both, nothing else was said.

Good thing, for Bernie's sake.

But now Kane had an inexplicable need to spend time with Presley out of the spotlight. It was dangerous—just as dangerous as sleeping beside her each night. But he couldn't seem to stop himself.

He didn't even want to try…

Kane watched her approach the barn across the drive,

his mouth watering at the faithful lie of her jeans over shapely hips. And those boots...

"What's in the bag?" he asked, desperate to distract himself.

Her grin was a little shy, a little sly. "My contribution to the picnic."

Kane peeked inside, and the heavenly aroma of fried chicken greeted him.

"It's not fast food," she offered, "but I hope you still like it."

Their eyes met, forming an almost tangible connection between them that set off warning bells in the logical part of Kane's brain. He shouldn't be this close. Shouldn't be this invested. It could lead to him taking over, stepping in where she didn't want—or need—him to go. Only he couldn't look away.

Her murmur was a little breathless. "Sounded like it was your favorite picnic food."

"Yes, ma'am." The obvious enjoyment in his tone made her smile even bigger.

"Then I suggest we get going before the food gets cold," she said.

He led her inside, where EvaMarie and Mason were already saddling their own horses. He and his brother had added more than a few horses since taking over this stable. For tonight's ride, Kane had chosen a mare with spirit that he knew Presley would appreciate. Nothing docile for her, but not enough of a challenge to make their ride hard work.

The goal was to relax, after all.

The four of them headed out the west side of the stables and along a well-worn path. The world around them was fresh with young leaves filling in the once empty spaces from winter. Kane soaked in the fresh air, still comfortably cool, and the sight of Presley swaying in her saddle in front of him.

As they arrived at a small clearing with a stream running through it, Presley exclaimed, "How pretty! I didn't realize y'all had water on the property."

"It starts at a spring up that hill," Mason explained. "Nice, huh?"

"If we had a spot this nice on our property, I'd never want to leave," Presley said.

"Oh, we don't, either," Mason said, winking over at EvaMarie.

Though he'd been teasing his fiancée, Mason was right. They didn't want to leave. And the day was just right for a picnic. The chicken went perfectly with the rest of the food EvaMarie had packed. They dipped their bare toes in the ice-cold water before indulging in dessert. Then they lay on blankets to stare up at the fluffy white clouds in the blue spring sky. It was peaceful. Kane hadn't felt this happy in a while—at least, outside Presley's arms.

Kane wasn't ready to end it and face reality, but work still had to be done. He and Presley were going to an event this weekend and a house party in a couple of weeks, so he needed to get ahead.

"This is where we used to have to run," Mason said as they rounded a curve near the end of their return trip, "since we were always cutting it close to your curfew. Remember, EvaMarie?"

"Lord, do I?" his fiancée confirmed. Her laughter subsided quickly. "Funny now, but I sure was scared Daddy would tan my hide if he found me gone, much less with you."

Things had turned out so well for his brother that Kane often forgot for long stretches that EvaMarie and Mason had dated when they were teenagers, leading to a very bitter breakup. Seeing them happy now, after many years apart, could almost make a man believe in destiny.

Almost.

"It usually became a race to see who could reach the edge of the woods first, without bursting from the tree line for everyone to see and hear," Mason explained to Presley.

"I won most often," EvaMarie bragged.

But Mason wasn't having it. "You did not."

"Yes, I did. I know these woods and this trail better than anyone," She glanced in Mason's direction with a brow raised in challenge. "Even you."

"Oh, really?"

Kane could see the slight tightening of Mason's hands on his reins. It was on now.

"Let's see about that," Mason yelled, then urged his horse to a full gallop.

EvaMarie gasped while Presley laughed. Both women pushed their horses to follow. Kane joined the chase, too.

Exhilaration flooded Kane's body. There was nothing like riding a horse at a full run. He and the animal moved as one, which wasn't surprising, since they'd done this many times in the past. He noticed Presley moving in tune with her horse, too. She was a natural horsewoman.

Kane had almost caught up with the others when he noticed they were approaching a part of the path that narrowed before opening onto the field near the stables. The three horses before him continued full throttle. His heart skipped a beat, fear taking over. The bottleneck wouldn't allow all three to pass. None of them seemed to be slowing down. Did Presley remember the narrow part from the ride out here?

Maybe not. She seemed to be urging her horse to go faster. Kane did the same, desperate to stop her even though he knew he couldn't reach her in time. EvaMarie suddenly reined in her horse, trying to make room for Presley, but there simply wasn't enough time.

Without a hitch, Presley guided the mare into a jump approach and sailed over the overgrown ravine that blocked her path. Kane missed seeing the landing somehow.

After a moment he realized he'd squeezed his eyes shut.

He flicked open his eyelids. Instead of the broken body he expected to find, he saw that Presley and her horse had continued on the path unharmed. Kane swore under his breath and swept past EvaMarie and Mason, both of whom had slowed significantly. By the time Kane emerged from the trees, Presley was reining in her mare near the stables.

Adrenaline, fear and anger pulsed through Kane, pushing him forward. He gave his horse its full head and sped across the sloping ground. Only as his horse rushed in close did he pull back hard on the reins and yell, "Presley! What the hell were you thinking?"

Startled, Presley and her mare shied away. But not quickly enough. Kane's horse bumped against the mare. Though Kane grabbed at Presley, he wasn't able to stop her from falling to the ground.

Fourteen

Presley glared up at the horse and man towering over her, wondering if her legs were long enough to kick him. But she couldn't risk hitting the horse instead.

"Why would you do that?" she demanded. The throb of pain in her backside annoyed her, but she was also grateful she'd landed where there was some padding. At least nothing had broken. "You know better."

He should. Kane had been around horses even longer than she had. Rushing one while yelling was a good way to get someone hurt. As it was, her mare had high-tailed it for the stables she knew were safe and quiet.

"Me?" Compared to her, Kane's voice was even. Deadly calm and cold. "You're the one who should know better. Taking a blind jump in unfamiliar territory."

Presley struggled to her feet despite protesting muscles. Tomorrow she'd be stiff and sore, but today she'd rather fight on her feet. After dusting off her legs and attempting to quell the urge to throw a tantrum like a toddler, she said, "It wasn't unfamiliar to me. I remembered it from the trek out."

On the periphery of her vision, Presley saw Jim, the Harringtons' stable manager, sprint from the stables in her mare's direction. He held something in his hand and his mouth moved, though she couldn't hear the words this far away. After a moment's hesitation, the mare allowed herself to be lured close enough for him to take control of her reins.

Several other stable hands exited the building. Great. An audience.

"Presley," EvaMarie gasped as she and Mason pulled their horses to a stop nearby, "are you okay?"

"She's fine," Kane snapped. "Despite making a stupid choice."

Presley felt her anger flare, and she put her fists on her hips. "I'm not stupid."

"I didn't say you were," Kane corrected. His jaw looked too tight to let the words out. "But that was a stupid, headstrong jump that didn't give a thought to safety—yours or the horse's."

Mason groaned.

Presley ignored him and waved toward her now captured mare. "Look who's talking. You yelling like that got me tossed on my rear. Is that safe, crazy man?"

"Kane," Mason said as he urged his gelding forward a few steps. "She's not Emily."

Brother glared at brother as understanding trickled through Presley, but that didn't make any of this okay. Fear like that had no place around these powerful animals. They rode all the time, but like cars, these animals could be dangerous under certain circumstances. Like now.

Kane needed to remember that. "He's right," Presley chimed in. "I'm not your ex-fiancée. I don't need you to take care of me, fix me or protect me. I've been handling those jobs myself my whole life."

Kane finally swung a leg over his horse's rump and dismounted. Then he faced Presley with his arms crossed tightly over his chest, biceps clearly defined through his T-shirt. She pretended not to notice…or be intimidated.

Now was not the time.

"I realize that, Presley," he said, his voice softening a little. "But that was a dangerous choice."

"No, it was fun. Until you ruined it." Presley wasn't sure why or where her next words came from, but she couldn't hold them back. "Kane, I took a risk. I'm fully aware of that. But it was a risk backed by knowledge."

Kane swept his hat from his head, giving her a better view of his impassive expression. His hands worked over the brim, crumpling it.

"I have a lifetime of knowledge, Kane," she continued. "That doesn't mean an accident won't happen, but I play it safe in every area of my life. This is the only one where I've learned to trust myself, my instincts. I won't start questioning them now."

Kane had taught her that, almost as much as her father. "I thought you trusted me, too…" she murmured.

As soon as the words reached him, Kane slapped the hat hard against his thigh. His jaw worked, clenching and unclenching in waves of tension that she could feel radiating off him. She wanted to relent, wanted to give in to his need to keep her safe. But somehow she knew if she did that, it would never end. Kane needed to remember the capable woman she was, not see his ex-fiancée every time he looked her way.

Then Kane shook his head with a jerk. "I don't know if I can live with that," he declared. Then he turned and walked away, leaving Presley with a throb in her heart that rivaled the one in her backside.

Presley wasn't sure if Kane would actually pick her up for the house party this weekend in Baltimore or not. She hadn't actually spoken with him since that day at the Harrington stables. Frankly, she'd expected to open the mailbox and find a bill and nullified contract from him any day now.

Then she'd received his terse call thirty minutes before he arrived. "I'll pick you up at noon" was the only warning she'd gotten.

Good thing she'd decided to pack—just in case.

There was a strained silence between them as he opened the car door for her and stowed her luggage in the trunk. He'd taken the luxury sedan instead of the usual SUV for the ride to the private airfield. It wasn't until they were settled and on the road that he said, "I wasn't sure you would go."

All you had to do was call and ask…

"I don't back down from my obligations."

"Is that what this is?"

It was certainly the only thing that had her in the car at the moment. Her emotions mixed and mingled even more forcefully than they had over the last week. Kane had finally broken through her wall of reserve—now she wanted nothing more than to rebuild it, to keep out one more person who would tell her how to live…but she couldn't.

So maybe she wasn't just here out of obligation.

After a long, tense moment, she finally murmured in the direction of the window she kept staring out, "I'm not sure."

Kane didn't speak. He only nodded his head.

That infuriated her. She was digging into her psyche, but he offered nothing of his own. And that wasn't acceptable. As the hot anger swept over her, she knew she needed answers. "What about you, Kane?"

He didn't look her way, but she saw his hands tighten on the steering wheel, knuckles turning white. "What do you want to know, Presley?"

Wasn't that a loaded question? There were so many things she'd wanted to ask for ages, but she stuck with the one question that was most pertinent to the moment.

"If this is only a business arrangement to you, why did you care if I fell?"

She sensed that wasn't the question he'd been expecting. She wouldn't be surprised if he chose not to answer, and for a long time he didn't. When he did speak, his voice was low and had an uneven rumble. "I would care if anyone got hurt, Presley, but especially you."

What did that mean? But he didn't offer anything else, and Presley had used all the courage she had to ask the one question.

Where did they go from here? The miles sped by in a flash of green hills. Kane turned on the radio, and soothing instrumental music filled the car. She doubted it was his first choice for ambience, but at least it calmed Presley's mood somewhat.

On the short flight out, Kane sat in the front with the pilot, leaving her alone with her spinning mind. Luckily she knew the family they were visiting well and had accepted their invite a while before she and Kane had become an item. The last thing she'd imagined was a weekend spent in the same room with him, this strained silence between them.

But when their hostess came to meet them under the portico while their luggage was being unloaded from the limo they'd taken from the airfield, an inkling of concern whispered through Presley.

"Hey, girl," LaDonna said as she hugged Presley. Her friendly greeting contradicted her strained smile. "So glad you made it."

LaDonna waited until after she'd greeted Kane before urging Presley a few steps away. "I didn't know Marjorie was coming."

Presley took in her hostess's worried expression. "Um, I didn't, either."

"She showed up several hours ago."

Presley squeezed her eyes shut for a moment, willing away a headache, then gave LaDonna a sympathetic look. "I'm so sorry. I hope that won't put you out."

"Well—" LaDonna glanced over her shoulder toward the doors as if to make sure the rest of the party—or the offending guest—hadn't shown up to listen. "The thing is, we have a full house this time. Every room is taken."

Great. Presley knew exactly what that meant. A weekend spent listening to her stepmother pick over every piece of clothing she'd brought to wear, or asking her a million times if Kane had picked out something she approved of. "Maybe I should just go home," she groaned.

"Why would you do that?"

Presley's eyes opened to see Kane's curious expression over LaDonna's shoulder.

"We've had an unexpected guest show up," LaDonna confessed.

"Marjorie," Presley sighed.

Kane's expression was neutral. "I realize she can be difficult, but why would that be reason to abandon ship?"

LaDonna glanced back and forth between them as if unsure what to say, but Presley wasn't in the mood to spell it out herself. "It's messed up our sleeping arrangements."

"Shouldn't." Kane's voice was more matter-of-fact than she would have expected considering the strain between them. She anticipated his next words as much as she dreaded them. "Presley will be staying in my room."

LaDonna's eyes widened, but thankfully she didn't

express disbelief or ask questions. She gave a polite smile. "That'll work, then."

But as LaDonna turned away from Kane, her wide eyes met Presley's. Her mouthed *oh my gosh* would have been comical if Presley didn't have so much weighing her down. She didn't want to make LaDonna uncomfortable—she'd always been a sweet woman, who had been a friend of Presley's mother and stayed in touch despite their living so far apart. Their shared investments in horse racing gave the families even better reason to continue their longstanding friendship. Presley didn't want to inconvenience her or spill the details of her currently troubled relationship—if one could call what she and Kane had a relationship. Deep down, she was very much afraid that's exactly what she wanted.

But now Presley had to figure out what to do with Kane—and the king-size bed they would soon share.

Fifteen

As Presley eyed him warily, Kane had the first urge to smile he'd felt in days. He wasn't sure why—the situation between him and Presley hadn't improved. But the look on her face implied he was a big bad wolf who would more than likely take advantage of her in their shared room.

By damn, she was probably right.

Not that she'd forgiven him for his behavior. She might be able to sleep with him, but her spirit wasn't quite willing. Kane had wavered about a solution to this problem—not to mention the cause—a lot over the last few days.

The answer wasn't making itself known quickly enough.

"Presley! You finally arrived."

The sound of Marjorie's voice when they were only halfway up the main staircase made Kane smother a groan. As if this weekend wasn't complicated enough... Marjorie wasn't his favorite person, but he tried to be polite to her. But add in the strain between him and Presley at the moment, and his patience with her step-mother was bound to be a little thin.

Presley seemed to feel the same way, as she said in a voice that held no warmth, "We didn't know you were going to arrive at all, Marjorie."

The older woman's titter set Kane's teeth on edge, as did the light glinting off all the sequins on her top.

"A last-minute decision," Marjorie assured them. "You shouldn't mind, Presley. After all, you have a place to sleep, don't you?"

The way she eyed Kane over her stepdaughter's shoulder made him distinctly uncomfortable. Either she didn't notice Presley's clenched jaw or she simply didn't care. Kane leaned toward the latter explanation.

Marjorie moved on to her next topic, one of her fa-vorites. "Please tell me you're on your way to dress for dinner, Presley. You shouldn't wear slacks in this type of company—"

"We are actually on our way to our suite," Kane in-terrupted, gesturing toward the man who waited at the top of the stairs with their luggage. "We'll be down for drinks once we're settled."

Presley didn't resist as he ushered her up the remain-ing steps. He handled the luggage while she crossed the suite to stare out the picture window overlooking the impressive gardens just coming into full bloom. Kane saw the waning sunlight darken to dusk in just a few minutes, giving the room a more intimate quality.

Knowing only that he had to reach her in some small way but unsure of how to go about it, Kane crossed to stand behind Presley. Though they weren't touching, standing like this reminded him of their trip to Louisville. He wanted to use his body to bend her just where he wanted her. Connect with her from head to toe, get them both too revved up to be able to go down to dinner.

But now wasn't the time to focus on sex. He could easily make her feel satisfied—but more importantly, he needed to make her feel respected. Their conversation in the car had told him that loud and clear.

So he did the one thing he didn't want to do. He started to speak. About his feelings.

"When my mother died, I was fifteen—" He paused for a deep breath. "No, it started before that. She'd been sick with cancer for almost two years before she was taken from us."

Presley shifted slightly, but he couldn't tell what she was thinking so he continued. With only a lamp on in the far corner of the room, there wasn't any light to see her reflection in the glass.

"My father worked full-time. Took care of all her medications, appointments, treatments…and he had me and Mason. But there are only so many hours in the day, and he had no relatives nearby to help him. Some of the neighbors would bring over food sometimes, but the longer an illness goes on, the easier it is for people to forget that you're in need."

He edged a little closer, drawn to her warmth.

"I wanted to help, so I begged my mom to teach me to cook the things she wanted to eat, whatever she thought she could keep down. Soups, mashed potatoes, pudding—soft foods to start. Soon I was making entire meals for everyone. I helped Mason with his homework every night so he wouldn't get behind. Took out the trash. Cleaned the bathrooms. Did laundry. Taking care of people just came naturally to me."

Kane sucked in another deep breath, momentarily distracted by the brush of his chest against Presley's back. The light scent of her hair, tied back into a thick ponytail, enticed him. He should stop talking before he revealed too much. Why didn't he stop talking?

"When Em fell, I ended up in the same place, the same head space. Like if I just worked hard enough, I could fix it."

"Since you didn't prevent it?"

The murmured words were quiet, but their impact was massive.

Kane's whole world tilted, leaving him dizzy. "Logically I knew I couldn't have stopped it, but that message didn't translate to my heart. So I tried to make up for it instead. Which didn't go over so well."

At all. Instead of bringing them closer, he'd driven Emily away. She'd needed space, time to heal…without him. The memories sent Kane back across to the dresser, pulling at his hair as he paced the expanse of the big room, his steps eerily silent on the plush carpets. "I should have handled it differently. Tempered my response to what she needed, what she wanted." He jerked to a halt, bracing his hands on hips. "It's just who I am, Presley."

"No."

Surprised, he braced himself to face her.

"That was your normal response on steroids. You felt yourself losing her, so you pumped it up."

And made myself into a fool.

"The truth, Kane, is that she probably would never have accepted your help."

"Why?"

Kane hated the plaintive note in his voice, yet it was also a relief to say the word out loud after listening to it echo inside his head for three years. Presley glanced back out the window, hesitating for long moments before she answered. Kane felt every second of that wait in his bones.

"I'll admit, I looked up the details of Emily's fall." Presley shrugged. "I was curious. But there were things that puzzled me for a while. How could someone so invested in horses go completely in the other direction after what was obviously an accident?"

"She wanted nothing more to do with them," Kane choked out. "When she left, she said she never wanted to see another animal or stable again."

"She moved to a big city, didn't she?"

Kane nodded.

"See, it could have gone the other way. There are lots of rehabilitation programs she could have worked with, helping her overcome her fears if she'd wanted to. But she didn't."

Presley took a few small steps closer to him. "And she couldn't ask you to give up your dreams, either, Kane. She wasn't pushing you away after her accident— she was pushing you in the direction of the future she knew you deserved. A future she couldn't handle being a part of anymore."

The truth hit Kane like lightning, jolting him from the inside out while freezing him in place. For so long, he'd had it in his head that Emily simply wanted nothing more to do with him, nothing to do with the essential parts of him. So those parts of him had to be buried— until the pressure of watching Presley accelerate toward that jump had his protective instincts spewing forth again like a shaken soda.

The implications whirled inside Kane's brain, making him dizzy. Through sheer force he shut down his mind. He could dwell on it later, when he was alone. Right now, Kane needed to focus on the uncomfortable present and lock away the devastating past for another time. "I thought I'd buried my triggers," he admitted, not acknowledging the turbulence inside himself. "Obviously I was wrong."

A weak apology at best, but all he could manage at the moment.

This time Presley advanced on him with sure steps. "You know, Kane, there's a difference between taking care of people and taking them over."

Wise woman. "I forget sometimes." With the best of intentions, but still…

"Then you'll just have to live with me putting you back in your place…when it's appropriate, of course."

Her moss-green gaze met his. A little vulnerable. A lot strong. And like a snap of his fingers, Kane's hesitation vanished.

He strode back to her, cupping her face to hold her captive for his kiss.

Once he started, there was no turning back. Passion, need and something deeper drove him forward. He made short work of stripping off their clothes. Her every gasp, every moan added an extra spark to his excitement. Luckily the bed was a soft landing place.

For a woman who worked so hard, Presley's skin was silky soft, drawing his hands, his mouth. Kane might have spent time dressing Presley, but undressing her was a unique pleasure. Her body was firm, muscled from her hard work. Her long, lean legs felt like heaven wrapped around Kane's hips.

He couldn't wait to have her there again.

Stepping to the edge of the bed, Kane made a place for himself between Presley's thighs. She was like the sweetest of treats laid out before him; Kane surveyed every inch before leaning over for a taste. He plumped her breasts with his hands. Her nipples tightened, begging for him. His kiss covered her delicate mounds, but he saved the little pink buds for last.

As he closed over one tip, Presley arched up to meet him. The dusky darkness of the room grew heavy with her moans and his ragged breath. She buried her hands in the thickness of his hair at the base of his skull, drawing him closer. He sucked at her tightened nipples until they darkened to rosy red.

Something about the feel of her, the sound of her, fit perfectly into the empty place in Kane's soul. He didn't want it, but there was no denying it. No way to stop himself from reaching out and taking her.

After slipping on a condom, he guided her legs around his waist. She locked her ankles together at the small of his back. Her core was wet and eager for him. Sliding inside felt even better than coming home.

It was just right.

The heat surrounding Kane lit an urgency inside him that he couldn't control. Spurred on by the pressure of her legs pulling him closer, he plunged deep inside her. His world stopped. All he knew was that he didn't want this to end. Didn't want to face the day when he would never again connect with Presley's very essence.

But his body wasn't interested in the emotions.

In and out, each thrust became an automatic drive to detonate their explosion. He leveraged his stance for maximum force, losing himself in the clutch of her hands and the exquisite pull of her body. Every thrust to the hilt threw them closer to the edge.

Kane knew he wanted nothing more than to jump into the free fall with Presley.

Just a minute more, and he felt the impact hit her, the clamp of her muscles around him a direct jolt to his own ecstasy. Kane felt suspended in a maelstrom of pleasure and pain before slowly returning to the softness of the woman beneath him and the solid foundation of the floor under his feet.

Never had reality felt so good.

* * *

Apparently she shouldn't have worried about that canceled contract.

Presley was pretty sure what they'd been doing upstairs shone from every pore on her face, but no one so much as hinted at it over dinner. Instead they all chatted pleasantly from cocktails to dessert, eager to meet the newest up-and-comer in the racing world when Presley introduced Kane.

As she watched him over the rim of her wineglass after dinner, she had the sinking feeling that Kane didn't truly need her anymore. He was far more comfortable in social situations than she was and quickly connected with whomever he met. Yes, she'd helped him gain entry to a couple of places it might have taken him longer to break into, but his name and reputation had spread rapidly.

When it was just the two of them, their connection felt almost tangible. Their lovemaking upstairs had left her with no barriers against her true feelings for him. But it was hard seeing him work a room full of people when her natural instinct was to hide in a corner. How long would it be before babysitting her grew old?

But she certainly wouldn't object to calling it an early night when she knew what was waiting for her upstairs.

LaDonna approached Presley's quiet corner. "Wow, Presley. I'm thoroughly impressed," she said as she eyed Kane, who was in conversation with a couple of high-powered horse brokers from Ireland.

"You should see him with his brother."

"I'd heard there were two of them," LaDonna said

with a playful wink. "Don't tell hubby that I'm salivating already."

She turned her focus fully on Presley. "I'm sorry about the mix-up with Marjorie, but I didn't know you and Kane were together when you asked for the invite. Why didn't you tell me, Presley?"

"I wasn't...sure." Heck, she still wasn't sure, if she admitted the truth.

"Are you happy?"

In some ways, very much. In others... But she couldn't tell LaDonna that. Instead she protected herself and the complicated situation she was in by saying, "Yes, why?"

"Well, I've tried hard not to malign Marjorie over the years."

Haven't we all?

"But as a mother, she was never quite right for you."

Marjorie's piercing laugh from across the room only punctuated that truth. Presley sighed, then said, "I'm glad I'm not the only one who saw it."

"Oh, your father had all the excuses for why you wouldn't take to his new wife, and Marjorie adopted them for herself from the beginning."

Presley tilted her head to the side, studying her stepmother in her sequined attire. Marjorie liked to glitter when she moved. "Do you think so?"

"I'm afraid so," LaDonna said. She indicated Presley's silky shirt and skirt with an elegant gesture. "And then I saw you like this, and I worried."

Presley glanced down, expecting to feel self-conscious to have someone talking about her new clothes, but she fell back into the knowledge that the outfit was lovely and felt good, too.

Then an unexpected vulnerability swept over her. "Do you think my mom would have liked it? Liked me?"

LaDonna stepped closer, reaching for Presley's ponytail and pulling it forward so it fell in a golden swath over her shoulder. "Most definitely, honey. But then again, she loved you in jeans and T-shirts, too. She didn't care much for fashion herself."

"She didn't?" Presley struggled to remember more about the mother she'd lost so long ago.

"Oh, no," LaDonna said with a soft smile full of memories. "She much preferred the comfort of her work pants. She dressed up when she had to, but she really wanted to be at ease most of the day. Formal clothes made her constantly worry about buttons coming loose, pockets poking out or the fabric twisting and not lying right. That stuff seemed to happen to her constantly."

Presley chuckled. "Like me."

"Like you." LaDonna shook her head. "I always wanted you to go with your gut, Presley. Still do. So would your mother."

Presley eyed the darkly handsome man across the room. Could she? Should she? Would she risk missing the most spectacular opportunity to ever come her way?

"You look beautiful, Presley. Don't forget that." Again LaDonna fingered her ponytail. "So like your mother. But most importantly, you finally look like you, comfortable in your own skin."

The little pep talk, which might have been insignificant to most people, stuck with Presley the rest of the night, prodding her into action. But it wasn't until she drifted in soft waves of approaching sleep, comfortable in Kane's arms, that she finally listened.

"I love you," she whispered, speaking the words that had been weighing on her conscience all day.

But when she finally slipped into slumber, his silence in return haunted her.

Sixteen

Kane's energy waned late the next afternoon, forcing him to excuse himself a few minutes early from the tour of the hosts' stables. They had some gorgeous animals, but Kane's focus was nonexistent at the moment. His uppermost need was to get a few minutes alone in their suite—some time to regain his equilibrium and figure out what the hell he should do now.

He'd been distracted since hearing Presley's whispered words the night before.

Kane had struggled to keep his body from reacting. He hadn't wanted her to think he was rejecting her precious gift, so he'd held perfectly still, letting her think he was already asleep.

He wasn't sure the ruse had worked. Presley had been subdued today, but that could also have been a natural consequence of Marjorie's over-the-top presence this weekend. The woman seemed to be everywhere they went. And her laugh—Kane had never known a sound that grated on his nerves so badly.

The thought of Presley having to manage this woman—her outrageous spending, constant criticism and, yeah, that laugh—all in an attempt to honor her father's wishes that Marjorie be supported and part of the Macarthur business made Kane's respect for the man take a nosedive. Of course, he'd probably known that Marjorie would sink within a year if Presley wasn't taking care of her.

As if his thoughts had conjured her, Kane heard that high-pitched, nail-scraping sound in the foyer at the end of the hall. He had a strong urge to turn around and find a back way upstairs, but that might take him a while in the unfamiliar expanse of the sprawling mansion. It was a gorgeous place but not the easiest to navigate.

Straight ahead was the quickest route.

The deep rumble of a male voice assured Kane that Marjorie wasn't alone. Perhaps he could squeeze through with just a quick acknowledgment. Except what he heard as he reached the spot where he could make out the actual words stopped him in his tracks.

"Sun is one of the most well-known and well-respected stallions in the industry, Ms. Macarthur. I'm shocked you don't have buyers lining up a mile deep."

"Oh, he's such a special animal—we don't want him to go to just anyone, so we're keeping the sale inquiries discreet, if you know what I mean."

Kane glanced around the corner to see a balding

gentleman he'd met at dinner the night before. Peter, he thought his name was. His vague race predictions and lack of hands-on knowledge left the distinct impression that Peter's wife was the brains of that operation.

The thought that Marjorie would try to sell Sun again, knowing the problems it had caused for Presley the first time, confounded Kane. The thought that she would sell such a beloved animal to a clueless stable owner was beyond his understanding.

"Well, I know he's a derby champ and renowned stallion," Peter said. "Y'all must want a pretty penny for him."

As she mentioned a figure almost twice what she'd charged Kane, his blood went from simmer to boiling. Somebody was getting bold. The fact that she'd do it while Kane and Presley were under the same roof proved she simply didn't care about the consequences.

Peter must have realized the price was over-the-top, because he shook his head.

"I do have a couple of other interested parties," Marjorie added for good measure.

"Still, I can't commit to that kind of money without consulting my wife. Will tonight be soon enough for an answer?"

Smart man. Before Marjorie could answer, Kane stepped from his hiding place into the foyer.

"That's a very good idea," he said, his voice echoing in the dome of the rotunda. "In the meantime, would you leave me with Ms. Macarthur for a moment? We have a pressing matter we need to discuss."

The man nodded, walking away with a smile and a

light whistle, completely unaware of the tension he left behind. Marjorie eyed Kane warily as he approached, and rightly so. His anger had grown to the point he couldn't hide it from his expression anymore.

"Doing a little business, Marjorie?" he asked, his voice quiet but forceful. He wasn't yelling, which was a good sign he was keeping his rage under control.

"I don't believe that's any of your business."

"Then you'd be wrong."

"No," she countered, her voice squeaking a little as he stepped closer. "No, I'm not wrong. You are not part of Macarthur Haven."

"Actually, you are wrong. You just tried to sell a horse that doesn't belong to you—for the second time."

"You must have misheard the conversation," she said, tilting her chin up.

"Really?" Kane mimicked Marjorie's high-pitched tone. "'I'll settle for that price, even though he's worth far more.'" He groaned, shaking his head. "Marjorie, that's twice what you charged me. I think you're getting a little greedy."

"Presley asked me to do it," Marjorie said, changing her tune. "She couldn't face doing it herself."

"Now you must think I'm ignorant." He stalked close enough to see the tremble of Marjorie's lower lip, but it didn't evoke any sympathy from him. "Presley loves that horse. She'd never sell him. That's the difference between us, Marjorie. I see Presley's heart, not just dollar signs."

That had her narrowing her gaze. "How in the world

could you know Presley better after two months than someone who has known her most of her life?"

"Maybe because I actually see her."

"Really?" Marjorie planted her hands on her well-endowed hips. "Well, doesn't that make you sound like an awesome guy? Even though we both know you're only dating her because of a contract. It's all a business deal."

"A business deal that happened because you stole her horse and sold it to me illegally."

"You're welcome."

"Excuse me?"

Her eyes widened, but Marjorie didn't back down. "You've gotten a lot out of that deal, haven't you? An awful lot."

"So you're just going to—what? Keep forcing her to fix your mistakes so you don't go to jail?"

Marjorie gasped. "Presley would never do that to me."

"No, she wouldn't," Kane agreed. "She also wouldn't put a stop to your illegal activities. So I'll make sure this never happens again."

Marjorie rolled her eyes. "And how do you plan to do that, tough guy?"

"I'll shut you down permanently. Your easy access will be over once I marry her."

That caught Marjorie's attention, her eyes widening. Then she stared over his shoulder, her look turning almost calculating. Kane didn't care what she planned to throw at him next. He had the upper hand now.

Only Marjorie wasn't afraid of delivering low blows that were only true in her own mind. "That's almost as bad as forcing her to give the money back and sign a contract saying you could escort her all over town, change how she looked, use our horse as stud—all with the added bonus of sex on demand."

"Marjorie!"

LaDonna's voice rang through the foyer, causing Kane to turn around with dread settling in his stomach like a stone. A group of half a dozen people watched from the doorway leading to the foyer.

Right in the middle of them stood a white-faced Presley.

"What do you want?"

Presley should have been surprised by LaDonna's words, but she wasn't. She could even make a guess as to who was at the door to their suite, since she had no doubt her stepmother would not be coming around to apologize. Heck, she probably wouldn't even go home but would continue to enjoy her weekend and the race tomorrow, oblivious to the looks and whispers cast her way.

No, the person at the door would definitely be Kane. He was too responsible to back down from his obligations.

Whatever he said must have been sufficient, because LaDonna glanced over her shoulder at Presley. The question in her expression was obvious, even though she didn't speak. Presley replied with a short nod.

LaDonna opened the door. "You have ten minutes," she warned before slipping outside herself.

Presley didn't turn around again to watch Kane cross

the room. It would remind her too much of the day before, and the stride of those long legs as he came for her. No. She couldn't face those memories right now.

Instead, she continued packing her suitcase.

"Leaving?" he asked.

Whatever she'd been expecting, it wasn't the soft, apologetic note in his voice.

"What's the point in staying?" she countered. "I can't be much help to you now that everyone knows I'm only with you because of a contract."

"Everyone?"

"This business is a pretty tight circle, as you well know," Presley said, tossing her extra pair of jeans into the suitcase with more force than necessary. "Word has already spread through the house by now, I'm sure. It will hit basically everywhere by the end of the race tomorrow."

Kane stepped close, halting the jerky movements of her hands with an arm across the front of her body. "Presley, I'm so sorry you had to hear that."

"Not as sorry as I am to be humiliated in front of people who have known me my entire life."

"That was not my intention. When I heard what she was doing—"

"You know what's even worse, Kane?" Glancing down, she noticed that the garment she kept worrying between her fingers was actually the silky nightgown she'd brought, knowing Kane would see her in it at some point. The old Presley would never have dreamed of wearing such a thing. Yet she'd thought about wearing it with excitement just two days ago.

She dropped it as if it burned her hands. "The worst part is that for some of them, this will explain exactly why you would choose to date someone as frumpy and uninteresting as me."

"Presley, that's not true."

She tilted her head up to meet his gaze. It hurt, having him this close, seeing the eyes that had stared her down with lust and laughter now dark and guarded.

"It is," she said softly. "They've known me forever as a smart businessperson, but not as a woman, Kane. I won't be able to pretend any longer that I'm truly a person you would want to be with for—" her breath shook for a moment "—for more than a business arrangement."

"Did you not hear what I said down there? None of this will be an issue anymore. I want to marry you, Presley."

She stepped away, unable to tolerate being this close to him while he said those words. Words she'd only dreamed of hearing. Words that she knew didn't hold the same meaning for him as they did for her. "Oh, I heard. And just a day ago I heard you tell me this was just about a contract."

"That wasn't me, sweetheart. That was you."

"I believe I told you I didn't know what this was really about, Kane. But that's changed."

"For me, too."

Kane didn't give any quarter this time. Gone was the man reaching out to her with soft words and kid gloves. Here was the man plowing over her boundaries with passion.

His forceful advance backed her up against the nearby wall. Not because she wanted to retreat, but because she was afraid of what one touch from him would ignite inside her. She was right to be afraid.

As Kane pressed close, her body ignited with heat and need. Presley was perilously close to losing her head in her desire for the things Kane could make her feel. Without her permission, her hands clasped his upper arms tight. She didn't protest as he buried his mouth against her neck.

Could she possibly live without this? How would she survive without the heady passion Kane had brought into her life? His body was backing her against the wall, mouth pushing aside the collar keeping his lips from her skin, hard need pressing into the cradle of her hips— and Presley wanted nothing more than to lose herself in the drive to ecstasy she'd only found with this man.

For long moments, she gave desire free rein. Her nails dug into his shirt. Her thigh clamped around the leg he slid between hers. When his mouth captured hers, she opened to him without hesitation. No matter how much she questioned Kane, this, she knew, he couldn't fake.

But even as he tasted and tempted her, she could not hold back the doubts of a lifetime. The fear of never being loved. The fear of never being pretty enough. The fear of never being truly seen. Doubts proven true again and again…until Kane.

If she didn't walk away now, new doubts would creep in, and she didn't want to live like that anymore. Didn't want to wonder if this was a business deal with a side dish of desire. No. She wanted love.

Somehow she found the strength to push him away, to step around him, to walk to the bed. Alone.

She snapped the suitcase closed. Whatever was left, LaDonna could ship to her. Right now, she simply had to get out before this humiliation gave way to the river of pain lurking beneath her careful control.

Pulling the suitcase from the bed, she rolled it toward the door. But she only made it halfway before she turned back. "What hurts even worse is that you think I would settle for a marriage that wasn't everything I deserve."

"And exactly what is that?" His soft tone was completely gone now.

"A man who respects me enough to trust I can fix my own problems, who will stand strong with me when I need him to and make decisions *with* me…not *for* me."

This time she didn't pause until she reached the door. "I'll have what's left of your money for the stud services returned to you in full by Monday."

Seventeen

The last person Presley expected to knock on their door on the following Wednesday evening was a lawyer she recognized from town. James Covey was well liked among the racing community, though he didn't actually own any horses. He was known to be fair, and Presley knew from seeing his name on the envelopes on Kane's desk that he was also the Harringtons' lawyer.

"Who is it?" Marjorie called from the hallway leading to the foyer. They'd been in the middle of dinner when the bell rang.

"No one," Presley called back as she opened the door.

"Ms. Macarthur?" the man asked, a more pleasant smile on his face than she would have anticipated.

"Mr. Covey?"

"I have a package for you from Mr. Kane Harrington."

She was shaking her head before he even finished. "I returned his money to him by cashier's check on Monday, delivered by courier," Presley said, anxiety churning in her stomach despite her certainty that she'd done more than was legally required of her. "Mr. Harrington should have no further need to contact me, much less through legal channels."

Unless he'd decided to insist on using Sun as a stud. She'd taken a significant hit to her business to return Kane's original sum to him in full. It hadn't been required according to their contract, but she'd wanted no further ties between them, which meant Sun would not be serving as a stud for the Harringtons' new stables. She hated to back out of any business deal, but right now, her sanity was more important to her than her bank account. Remembering that it was only a temporary loss that the business would recover from helped.

No matter how much writing that check had stung.

"I cannot say why Mr. Harrington chose this way to contact you, ma'am," the lawyer said.

Again, Presley wondered about his benign expression. Either he was quite good at masking his true thoughts or the envelope didn't contain a subpoena or any other legal threat.

He continued, "I was simply instructed to deliver it to you personally."

Presley barely registered his parting "Good evening" as she studied the oversize envelope in her hands. It was creamy white with the lawyer's logo in one corner and her name scrawled in Kane's bold handwriting across the center. Just seeing the strong curves and almost sharp lines brought to mind an image of watching him write. Kane's script wasn't messy, like a lot of men's. Instead it was indicative of his personality, daring and smooth and elegant.

No matter his family's class growing up, Kane had a pride and expectation of quality that had shone through consistently. His quality of character had come through again in the fallout from the gossip about their original contract. From the gossip Marjorie had shared, when questioned at a cocktail party the other night he'd refused to speak about contracts that were nobody's business but the parties involved.

At least Kane was protecting her. The same couldn't be said for her stepmother. Presley's threat to once more talk to their lawyer seemed to have kept Marjorie quiet—for now.

"What's taking so long?" Marjorie asked from her elbow, startling Presley. She hadn't realized Marjorie had joined her.

"It's nothing. Just some business papers."

Her stepmother studied the envelope, but Presley knew she wouldn't know where it was from, since the Harrington name didn't appear on it. She set the package on a side table and went back to the dining room as if it were truly unimportant, but it wasn't as easy to put the contents out of her mind. Still, she forced herself to wait until Marjorie had finished eating and retired to her room for the evening. She had a lunch date the next day that it would take her all night to prepare for, she said.

Presley still couldn't imagine putting that much thought and time into her appearance, even if she was enjoying her new clothes. Mrs. Rose had helped her build quite a closet full. Though she wasn't looking forward to any social events any time soon. She imagined whatever she wore from now on would be examined and talked about, but she refused to go backward.

She'd just have to learn to deal with it with a straight face.

Her hands trembled as she took the envelope to the privacy of her office. Why? She had nothing to be concerned about. She'd fulfilled her obligation to Kane per their contract and returned everything to him in full. Why he was contacting her now, she had no idea.

But this was business. She needed to suck in her emotions and handle whatever needed to be done.

The first thing she noticed as she dumped the contents onto her desk was the check she'd had delivered to Kane on Monday. Only now it was stamped with a big black "Void" across the front.

Her heart started to pound in earnest. If he was refusing her payment, then he must want something else. Although what that something would be, she couldn't imagine. She'd given him his freedom. He should be grateful.

She picked up the sheaf of papers and began to read the top page. The impersonal *Ms. Macarthur* on the Harrington Farms letterhead didn't bode well.

Receipt of your cashier's check surprised me, even though you warned me it would be arriving. In truth, the money does not interest me, so I am returning it to you in the form of a voided check.

Why? Why would the money not interest him? Unless he thought there was some other way she needed to fix whatever damage might come to his business after the weekend's revelations made the rounds.

In the interest of opening further negotiations, I'm having my lawyer deliver a new document for you to consider. Not a contract, per se. More of an agreement.

This is the only agreement I am willing to entertain, with mild adjustments at your discretion. I will only accept this document if it is returned by you, in person, at your convenience.

Sincerely, Kane Harrington

What kind of jerk thought he could dictate the terms of their further business dealings after humiliating her in public? Presley flipped to the next page with such force that the cover letter tore.

It is the wish of Kane Harrington to enter into a romantic agreement with Presley Macarthur that includes, but is not limited to, living in the same home, discussing business and personal interests with each other, being seen in public together, and, in general, allowing all intimate activities that would be acceptable and agreed upon between two people who wish to spend their lives together. This agreement may or may not include marriage, at Ms. Macarthur's discretion, but Mr. Harrington would prefer that a permanent romantic agreement occur in order to publicly acknowledge his devotion and love for her.

In acknowledgment of previous behaviors, Mr. Harrington agrees not to bring undo public attention to Ms. Macarthur in any way except during a wedding ceremony, should both parties agree. Should their previous contract ever be mentioned to him by interested parties, he will explain in no uncertain terms that their business arrangement was for the couple's mutual benefit and was of no concern to anyone but the two of them.

It is Mr. Harrington's responsibility to support and encourage Ms. Macarthur, but to in no way make her decisions for her. He agrees to only come to her defense when she is not able to defend herself, and to discuss disagreements in a calm and approachable manner, rather than dictating.

Mr. Harrington acknowledges that Ms. Macarthur is a smart, sexy woman who has years of knowledge and business acumen on her side. He will trust her to use that knowledge to her benefit and for her safety, and he will do his best not to infringe on that in any way.

It is Mr. Harrington's utmost wish to spend the rest of his life with Ms. Macarthur, loving her and caring for her to the best of his ability, in hopes that she will help him to become the best man to meet her needs and desires for all of eternity. He requests that she support him during all of his future business decisions, offering her knowledge as he builds Harrington Farms to the scale he and his brother have always dreamed possible.

All previous agreements between Mr. Harrington and Ms. Macarthur are furthermore null and void, requiring no further obligations to be fulfilled.

The rest of the page went on with more details that blurred through the tears in her eyes, but it was the last bit, handwritten across the bottom, that struck her the most: *Presley, I admit I'm hopelessly addicted to you—your strength, your common sense, your professional expertise and most of all the way you give me your all when you are with me. I want to be brave, to move on from the past into the most incredible future I could imagine—a future with you. Be brave with me. I need you... Kane.*

It took Presley an entire day to respond to Kane's package—and Kane felt every minute from sunrise to sunset in the depths of his soul.

When he glanced out the window of his office at Harrington Farms and saw her truck in the driveway, his heart stopped for a beat. Part of him wanted to know her answer. Part of him didn't want to know if the answer was negative. He could just live in this anxious limbo for eternity, right?

When EvaMarie showed her into the room, Presley's expression didn't offer him any glimmers of hope. Her poker face was pretty good. She held the envelope he'd had James Covey deliver lightly in one hand. Despite inheriting an incredible sum of money, Kane was a realist. His life had been hard, often struck by tragedy. He had a feeling today would be the hardest of them all.

In business, he could always push through and turn things around. On the personal side, Kane knew life didn't work that way.

"I received your package—" she started, but that wasn't where Kane wanted to begin.

"Before that, please accept my apology."

He must have disrupted a script in her head, because Presley blinked for a moment. "What?" she asked.

"Before we go any further," Kane said again, "I would like for you to accept my apology."

Another slow blink.

"I did not mean to embarrass you or harm you, Presley. I realize my instincts to protect you had those unintended consequences, and I'm very, very sorry. No matter what happens today, I hope you know that."

"I do, Kane," she said, sounding dishearteningly formal. "I know you saw what was happening and only wanted to protect me from further harm. Thank you."

"I never would have said any of that if I had realized I had an audience."

She nodded, her pale cheeks flushing beneath his gaze. It was the first sign of emotion he'd seen. That was a little encouraging, at least.

Then she lifted the envelope. "This told me a lot. But it also brought up some questions."

"How so?"

"Kane…" She glanced away, her delicate throat

working. "I want to believe, because of this, that my fears are unfounded. But I can't quite let them go."

He clenched the edge of his desk, desperate to go to her. To wrap her up in his arms and prove to her that fears didn't matter, that the past didn't matter. But that wasn't what she needed—and for once he wasn't letting his emotions push him into action.

With a deep breath, he let her lead by saying, "What can I do to help?"

"Tell me, Kane. I need to know that I wasn't just a fun bonus to a business deal you needed. That I wasn't just a doll to be dressed up to make you look good. A woman you would have defended no matter who I was personally."

Damn. "I'm sorry, Presley. I won't tell you that."

Her businesslike mask was stripped away in an instant, and Kane saw the blatant pain he'd caused her in full color. But he couldn't back down now.

"I won't tell you that because you know, deep down, none of that is true. It never has been. We may have started this as a business arrangement, but it turned into something else quicker than wildfire."

His unexpected answer grabbed her attention, pulling her focus back to him. "Before I knew it, I was in love with a tomboy who knows horses inside and out, a daughter who is doing her best to fulfill her father's last wishes, and a woman who is as beautiful outside as she is on the inside."

This time he let himself stand, let himself circle his desk and take the seat next to her. Tears welled in her eyes as she leaned toward him. "I can't change who I am, Kane."

"I know."

"I don't want to spend my life with someone who can't accept me the way I accept me. My father—he gave me a life of opportunities to explore my own interests. Horse camp and 4-H club and jeans, but there was always a persistent undercurrent of pressure to be more like the other girls. The casual remarks that told me he wished I had preferred cotillion and cheerleading."

"And you shouldn't have to live like that," Kane said.

He brushed away the single tear that trembled on her cheek. Then he pushed aside a few strands of the gorgeous blond hair she'd left loose around her face.

"I felt that, at Mrs. Rose's, you saw me," she said, her voice barely above a whisper. "You helped me find what worked for me, instead of dressing me up to fit your image. I was just…" She shrugged weakly. "I was afraid to trust that experience when so many people told me it couldn't be right."

He cupped his hand against her cheek. "Presley, I can't spend a lifetime reassuring you that you're the woman for me. My presence, my fidelity, my love are all the proof you need. You'll simply have to trust me, give me time to prove it to you."

There was no holding back from meeting her lips with his, a kiss that was just as much a pledge as it was a pleasure.

"Just like you can't spend a lifetime reassuring me that your every decision will keep you safe and sound.

I have to trust that your knowledge and skills will bring you home to me safely."

"I don't want you to live in fear," she murmured against his lips.

"I've been there enough," he agreed, "and I'm ready to move on."

"I do understand, though."

Pulling back, he held her glistening gaze for long moments. "Understand what?"

"Why you behaved like you did. I just didn't see it at the time." Her deep breath gave her next words the air of a confession. "You wouldn't have been so upset about the jump if you didn't care. You wouldn't have defended me so fiercely, without thought to who was listening, if some pretty strong feelings weren't involved."

"How do you know?"

Her smile captured his heart. "Because I feel the same way."

Kane couldn't hold back. His lips covered hers as he sought both to take and be taken. Her soft surrender empowered him. Yet he strove in every way to please her, to show her the love he'd never thought to experience after a lifetime of pain.

When they finally came up for air, Kane was surprised to hear Presley say, "I think our agreement needs a new clause."

"What's that?"

"That whenever fear starts to take hold, we have to tell the other immediately."

He liked that plan. "Sounds good."

"And we have to find the best way possible to calm

those fears and move past them, without letting them rule our world."

If he wasn't mistaken, judging by the increased color in her cheeks and the sexy arch of her brow, the little negotiator in front of him had some pretty interesting ideas how to do that already. He liked this plan more and more.

"I'll have James draw that up immediately." He stood, anxious to be closer to her, to feel her body against his own. "Do you have any other demands?"

She stood as well. "Only one."

"What's that?" he asked, not surprised that his voice had deepened with her nearness.

"We go somewhere more private—" she glanced around his office with a blush and a shy smile "—and spend the next few hours exploring exactly what else this merger might need to be successful. Every possible avenue should be explored."

Yes, ma'am. "Good plan. I have a few ideas we should definitely discuss."

Epilogue

A year later

"Push, girl. Push!"

Mason's cheering scraped over Presley's nerves, followed by the more soothing, soft encouragement offered by Kane. "Come on, girl. You can do it."

The men stood side by side, coaching, sweating and just generally making a mess of themselves. Any woman could have told them it wouldn't help.

"I think she knows what she's doing," Presley said through clenched teeth. Being this close to a birthing while her own belly was swollen with her first child set her on edge for the first time in her life.

Mason smirked at her over his shoulder, not realizing

how close to physical injury that put him. "Woman's intuition and all that jazz, huh?"

Presley wasn't amused. "You say that during labor and you'll likely find yourself kissing the floor," she assured him.

"You wouldn't do that to me, would you, love?" he asked, eyeing EvaMarie as she rubbed a hand over her distended belly in slow circles.

"Maybe…" She smiled sweetly, but there was a slight menace beneath the surface Mason didn't seem to notice. "You remember those films they made us watch in birthing class, right?"

Mason grimaced. "Don't remind me."

"There are certain parts you better remember pretty darn well, buddy," EvaMarie said. Presley had a feeling he'd be needing that knowledge sooner than he realized. If she wasn't mistaken, EvaMarie had been having contractions for the past two hours, at least. Mason had been too focused on the horse to notice.

Kane eyed Presley's matching tummy with a wary expression. "Is it too late to change our minds?"

"You bet, mister," Presley said.

The horse in the stall beyond the men whinnied, reminding everyone why they were actually here in the stables in the early hours of the morning. Mason yawned wide. "I could use some coffee," he said.

Presley glanced over at EvaMarie. "Oh, you're definitely going to hurt him in the delivery room," she said.

EvaMarie gave her a knowing look.

"Here it comes," Kane interrupted.

They rushed to the half door, peering inside as the mare

made her final push to get her baby into the world. A vet watched from inside the stall, and Jim stood next to him. They weren't taking any chances with this mare or her foal.

She was special.

She was also a very good mommy, moving right away to free her baby from his sac and ensure all was well. As the four of them stood long minutes later watching the foal struggle to his feet for the first time, Presley's eyes filled with tears. "Look at that," she breathed.

The foal was the spitting image of his sire.

Kane rubbed her aching back. "Sun's first foal here at Harrington Farms."

Bending over with a little difficulty, EvaMarie lifted wineglasses and two bottles from a cooler nearby. "Time to celebrate," she said.

Mason filled the men's glasses with champagne while Kane did the same with a nonalcoholic version for the women. They all shared bright smiles as the gentle sounds of the mother and baby getting to know each other wafted around them.

"To new beginnings," Mason said as they lifted their glasses for a toast.

"And a future without fear," Kane added, resting his hand on Presley's tummy.

They clinked glasses and drank, knowing that they were doing everything they could to make both of those pledges come to pass. Before their glasses were even empty, EvaMarie gasped, jerking her hand so the last of her drink spilled to the floor.

"Sweetheart, are you okay?" Mason asked.

The women shared a look, then Presley started to

giggle. Watching Mason go through this was going to be quite amusing.

"What's so funny?" Kane asked.

Presley eyed her brother-in-law with a touch of glee. "I think someone is going to experience an up-close version of labor a little sooner than he thought."

EvaMarie nodded. "My water just broke."

Mason's eyes went even wider. "Are you serious?"

"Don't worry, brother," Kane said, slapping Mason on the back. "The vet's already here."

"Oh, hell, no," he said, grabbing EvaMarie's hand and rushing her out the door.

Well, as fast as one could rush a pregnant woman in labor.

But all amusement was gone later that night as Presley stood holding her new niece, Kane's arms wrapped tightly around her. Mason lay crowded against EvaMarie in the hospital bed across the suite as the two tried to catch a little bit of sleep before visiting hours were over.

"She's beautiful," Presley whispered, slipping her finger against the baby's palm. Her heart felt like it was overflowing. Even asleep, the child gripped her as if holding her hand. "Bless her heart. She's all tuckered out." She smiled at her husband, the father of the child they would soon have. "New beginnings are hard work," she said.

Kane kissed her softly, then stared into her eyes. "They definitely are...but they're more than worth it."

* * * * *

Don't miss any of these dramatic
southern romances from Dani Wade:

REINING IN THE BILLIONAIRE
EXPECTING HIS SECRET HEIR
THE RENEGADE RETURNS
THE BLACKSTONE HEIR
A BRIDE'S TANGLED VOWS

Available now from Harlequin Desire!

***

If you're on Twitter, tell us what you think
of Harlequin Desire! #harlequindesire

COMING NEXT MONTH FROM

HARLEQUIN *Desire*

Available July 3, 2017

#2527 THE BABY FAVOR
Billionaires and Babies • by Andrea Laurence
CEO Mason Spencer and his wife are headed for divorce when an old promise changes their plans. They are now the guardians for Spencer's niece...and they must remain married. Will this be their second chance, one that leads to forever?

#2528 LONE STAR BABY SCANDAL
Texas Cattleman's Club: Blackmail • by Lauren Canan
When sexy former rodeo champion turned billionaire Clay Everett sets his sights on his spunky secretary, he's sure he holds the reins in their affair. Until he learns Sophie Prescott is carrying his child. Now all bets are off!

#2529 HIS UNEXPECTED HEIR
Little Secrets • by Maureen Child
After a fling with a sexy marine leaves Rita pregnant, her attempts to reach the billionaire are met with silence...until now! Brooding, reclusive Jack offers to marry Rita—in name only. Will his new family give him the heart to embrace life—and love—again?

#2530 PREGNANT BY THE BILLIONAIRE
The Locke Legacy • by Karen Booth
Billionaire Sawyer Locke only makes commitments to his hotel empire—until he meets fiery PR exec Kendall Ross. Now he can't get her out of his mind—or out of his bed. But when she becomes pregnant, will he claim the heir he never expected?

#2531 BEST FRIEND BRIDE
In Name Only • by Kat Cantrell
CEO Jonas Kim must stop his arranged marriage—by arranging a marriage for himself! His best friend, Vivian, will be his wife and never fall in love, or so he thinks. Can he keep his heart safe when Viv tempts him to become friends with benefits?

#2532 CLAIMING THE COWGIRL'S BABY
Red Dirt Royalty • by Silver James
Rancher Kaden inherited a birth father, a powerful last name and wealth—none of which he wants. His pregnant lover, debutante Pippa Duncan, has lost everything due to a dark family secret. Their marriage of convenience may undo the pain of their families' pasts, but will it lead to love?

YOU CAN FIND MORE INFORMATION ON UPCOMING HARLEQUIN® TITLES, FREE EXCERPTS AND MORE AT WWW.HARLEQUIN.COM.

HDCNM0617

Get 2 Free Books,
Plus 2 Free Gifts—
just for trying the Reader Service!

HARLEQUIN *Desire*

*After a fling with a sexy marine leaves Rita pregnant,
her attempts to reach the billionaire are met with
silence...until now! Brooding, reclusive Jack offers to
marry Rita—in name only. Will his new family give him
the heart to embrace life—and love—again?*

*Read on for a sneak peek of
LITTLE SECRETS: HIS UNEXPECTED HEIR
by USA TODAY bestselling author Maureen Child.*

Jack didn't make a habit of coming here. Memories were
thick and he tended to avoid them, because remembering
wouldn't get him a damn thing. But against his will, images
filled his mind.

Every damn moment of that time with Rita was etched
into his brain in living, vibrant color. He could hear the
sound of her voice. The music of her laughter. He saw the
shine in her eyes and felt the silk of her touch.

"And you've been working for months to forget it," he
reminded himself in a mutter. "No point in dredging it up
now."

What they'd found together all those months ago was
over. There was no going back. He'd made a promise to
himself. One he intended to keep.

It was a hard lesson to learn, but he had learned it in the
hot, dry sands of a distant country. And that lesson haunted
him to this day.

But Jack Buchanan didn't surrender to the dregs of fear, so he kept walking, made himself notice the everyday world pulsing around him. Along the street, a pair of musicians was playing for the crowd and the dollar bills tossed into an open guitar case. Shop owners had tables set up outside their storefronts to entice customers and, farther down the street, a line snaked from a bakery's doors all along the sidewalk.

He hadn't been downtown in months, so he'd never seen the bakery before. Apparently, though, it had quite the loyal customer base. Dozens of people—from teenagers to career men and women—waited patiently to get through the open bakery door. As he got closer, amazing scents wafted through the air and he understood the crowds gathering. Idly, Jack glanced through the wide, shining front window at the throng within, then stopped dead as an all-too-familiar laugh drifted to him.

Everything inside Jack went cold and still. He hadn't heard that laughter in months, but he'd have known it anywhere. Throaty, rich, it made him think of long hot nights, silk sheets and big brown eyes staring up into his in the darkness.

He'd tried to forget her. Had, he'd thought, buried the memories; yet now they came roaring back, swamping him until Jack had to fight for breath.

Even as he told himself it couldn't be her, Jack was bypassing the line and stalking into the bakery.

Don't miss
LITTLE SECRETS: HIS UNEXPECTED HEIR
by USA TODAY *bestselling author Maureen Child,*
available July 2017 wherever
Harlequin® Desire books and ebooks are sold.

www.Harlequin.com

HARLEQUIN® *Desire*

AVAILABLE JULY 2017
LONE STAR BABY SCANDAL
BY
LAUREN CANAN

PART OF THE SIZZLING
TEXAS CATTLEMAN'S CLUB: BLACKMAIL SERIES

When sexy former rodeo champion turned billionaire Clay Everett sets his sights on his spunky secretary, he's sure he holds the reins in their affair. Until he learns Sophie Prescott is carrying his child. Now all bets are off!

AND DON'T MISS A SINGLE INSTALLMENT OF

TEXAS CATTLEMAN'S CLUB:
BLACKMAIL

No secret—or heart—is safe in Royal, Texas...

The Tycoon's Secret Child
by *USA TODAY* bestselling author Maureen Child

Two-Week Texas Seduction by Cat Schield

Reunited with the Rancher
by *USA TODAY* bestselling author Sara Orwig

Expecting the Billionaire's Baby by Andrea Laurence

Triplets for the Texan
by *USA TODAY* bestselling author Janice Maynard

A Texas-Sized Secret
by *USA TODAY* bestselling author Maureen Child

Lone Star Baby Scandal
by Golden Heart® Award winner Lauren Canan

AND

August 2017: *Tempted by the Wrong Twin* by *USA TODAY* bestselling author Rachel Bailey
September 2017: *Taking Home the Tycoon* by *USA TODAY* bestselling author Catherine Mann
October 2017: *Billionaire's Baby Bind* by *USA TODAY* bestselling author Katherine Garbera
November 2017: *The Texan Takes a Wife* by *USA TODAY* bestselling author Charlene Sands
December 2017: *Best Man Under the Mistletoe* by Jules Bennett